At that moment, Schwab felt himself reach out—not physically; the Ernest Schwab at the end of the couch continued to stand motionless over the reclining figure. He felt, distinctly, a moment of contact, mind to mind, then an overwhelming rush of data from the other mind: emotions, thoughts, memories—most of all, memories. Somehow, he knew the man was Jeremy Morris, governor of the Earth colony on Paria. He knew he was in Morris's mind, following the man's life back through the years of college, school, back to the earliest moments of Morris's childhood and at last to what seemed like a few moments of warm security. The information, everything Morris had been or done, hurtled past in unbelievable complexity; yet at the same time in utter clarity. Schwab was simultaneously aware of the rush of the collapsed years through his mind and the few seconds it took to occur, the blinding intensity of the images from Morris's mind and the dull reality of the office around them. Mentally, he struggled, trying futilely to break contact, to separate his mind from the mind of the man on the couch. The effort had no effect. The images and sensations still rushed past.

In another part of his own mind, Schwab knew what was happening. He knew Morris's mind was being emptied, cleared of its every memory—that Morris would be nothing but an empty shell, a husk, shucked and abandoned. He knew he was responsible for what was happening as surely as if he had willed it. Yet, try—strain against the flow of memory—as he would, he could do nothing to halt it.

MEET THE AUTHOR

Steve Hahn is a man in what he describes as "the ripe years of late youth," somewhere between 28 and middle age. He lives outside Phoenix with his wife and two children in an adobe house he built himself. After receiving his B.A. in philosophy from U.C.L.A., he moved to Phoenix and became administrator of the Phoenix Small Claims courts. This job still occupies his weekdays. On weekends, he writes science fiction and is an avid eponymist. He has been involved in several conventions, most notably as Guest of Honor at Bulcon in Bulfinch, New Mexico.

Mindwipe! is Steve Hahn's first LASER BOOK

STEVE HAHN

MINDWIPE!

Cover
Illustration by
KELLY
FREAS

Toronto • New York • London

MINDWIPE!

A LASER BOOK/first published December 1976

ISBN 0-373-72051-3

Printed in U.S.A.

CHAPTER 1

"If I had some idea what was happening," said Schwab, folding the last of his shirts into his planet bag, "I'd know what to take with me. Do they want me down there for an hour? A day? A month?"

Boatswain Wheelwright shrugged. "Search me. I'm just passing along the message. They want you on the surface. You can give me a call once you're there and tell me how long you think it will be."

Schwab nodded and thumbed closed the seam on the bag. He had enough work to do aboard the *Chanticleer* to keep him busy for a month. In particular, the starboard quadrant debris sensors, used between hyperspace jumps, were working on backup systems. They had failed shortly before the *Chanticleer* took up a parking orbit around Paria. Schwab had hoped to use the time in orbit to make the necessary repairs.

He told Wheelwright to make sure a crew did a thorough systems check on the starboard sensors and hefted the planet bag over his shoulder. In the low artificial gravity of the *Chanticleer*, the bag—over 25 kilos Earth normal—rode easily. He left his cabin and started for the aft air lock, promising Wheelwright he would call the ship as soon as possible. Whoever had sent the order to bring Schwab to the surface had failed to use the proper identification code. Still, Schwab had been a ship hand long enough to ignore technicalities. People who stood on that sort of minor irregularity were usually dubbed "uncooperative" and passed over for higher positions. Paria's human colony was small enough to make finding whoever sent the order a simple matter. With only one hotel, all he had to do was check in and wait to be contacted.

At the aft air lock, he joined a work crew preparing to drop to the surface to repair a grounded ore shuttle. Pyraclore ore, supplying niobium and tantalum to industries around the federation, was the Parian colony's only reason for existence. During the infrequent visits of ships like the *Chanticleer*, a long-haul interstellar freighter, the colony came alive, filling shuttles with the ore collected between visits and transferring it to the spacecraft. The rest of the time, the human colony slept, the Parians themselves doing most of the work.

The air lock door hissed slightly—the shuttle and ship pressures equalizing—and opened. Schwab followed the work crew inside, taking one of the cushioned acceleration chairs at the edge of the group. During the half-hour trip to the surface, he found himself becoming the center of attention or, more precisely, the butt of a prolonged joke. After a general discussion of the matter, the work crew assured Schwab he must be well thought of in the upper levels of Diversicorp, the Earth-based corporation that owned both the *Chanticleer* and the mining operation on Paria. A normspace drive technician named Eaton seemed particularly amused by the idea and kept at it most of the way down.

"Yes sir-ree, Ernie, they sure must like you on top. You don't see the brass letting me or Al Grogen or Billie Barmclinsky take our planet leave down in that dust bowl, do you? They must think you're pretty special. They've probably got one of them Parian critters all saddled up to take you on the grand tour, you being such an important person and all. I hear them critters smell like burnt insulation."

"That isn't what *I* hear they smell like," shouted Barmolinsky.

Eaton cast Barmolinsky a look of mock reproach. "What do you know about it, 'Linsky? Last time we were here, I talked to Curly Curtis. He works down there nowadays. He said they smelled like burnt insulation."

For the first time, Schwab took an interest in the conversation. "Curly Curtis is down there?"

Eaton nodded. "Last I heard. Why he likes it I don't know. Know him?"

"I worked with him on the old *Reynard*."

"Anyway," continued Eaton, returning to his joke, "whatever them critters smell like, it's bad. Old Curly was definite about that. When you get back to the ship, Ernie, we may not get too close to you for a week or so, but don't worry about it. Once the smell wears off, you'll be okay. You just have a good time planetside." Eaton turned his head toward Barmolinsky. "Hey, 'Linsky, what do they do for a good time down there?"

"I hear they sit around a lot. Must be pretty exciting."

"That must be the part old Curly Curtis likes so much."

The ribbing continued for the rest of the trip. Schwab either ignored it or took what he could not ignore good naturedly. In their position, he would not have missed the opportunity to do the same thing.

The shuttle, guided from ship to planet entirely by computer, touched the upper atmosphere and changed course. Inside, the change was almost imperceptible. The men swayed slightly in their chairs. Schwab spent most of the time before touchdown trying to guess at the purpose of his visit. In spite of Eaton's suggestion, Paria was not the kind of planet anyone would voluntarily choose for planetside leave. Consequently, only business took people to the surface. Perhaps he was being transferred to another ship, one due in this sector after the *Chanticleer* departed. Perhaps the message was too personal to send through the normal communications system. There was only one solution—wait and see.

The shuttle touched down with only a slightly more perceptible jolt. The gravity stabilizers switched off and Schwab felt the .8 Earth-normal gravity of the shuttle replaced by something like Earth-normal. He waited for the work crew to file out, then followed them through the short tunnel to a set of stairs.

His first sight of Paria proved to be both disappointing and expected. Disappointing because the place seemed to consist of an expansive plain, occasionally broken by a bump of some sort—the word "anthill" kept coming to mind—and the human concession, a small cluster of buildings under a static field. The shuttleport, if it could be called that, consisted of even less—there were a few buildings to house equipment and an area set aside for shuttle landings.

Schwab returned his attention to the work crew, now clustered around a man standing next to a dustrover. The balloon-tired vehicle came up to the man's chest. Schwab recognized him immediately as Curly Curtis.

Curtis saw Schwab and, breaking away from the work crew, walked toward Schwab, a wide grin on his face.

"Ernie, how the hell have you been?"

They shook hands and started toward the dustrover. "Good, Curly. I see they've got you playing chauffeur. Quite a comedown from starship hand."

"It's only temporary. Just long enough to get you to the hotel. When I heard you were coming down, I decided I needed a break from supervising the ore transfer. Ah, here we are." Curtis gestured at the dustrover. "Ever ridden in one of these things?"

"Once or twice."

"You feel like you're sloshing around in a boat."

They climbed in. Curtis punched out the ignition code on the dashboard computer. The independent motors in each wheel whined momentarily, then engaged. The dustrover lurched forward, heading for the concession at a creeping five kilometers an hour. Schwab commented on the breakneck speed.

Curtis looked offended. "This is the fastest one we have around here. When nothing else is going on—which is most of the time—we have turtle races with them." Curtis patted the dash. "This baby comes in first every time."

"Turtle races?"

"Set them on automatic—" Curtis pointed across the plain at the mounds "—pick a bump and see which one gets there first."

"Someone said Paria was an exciting place."

"The hectic pace does get to you sometimes."

After rehashing old times and catching up on old acquaintances, the conversation turned to Paria and Curtis's life there. He described the concession's general layout to Schwab, going into more detail than Schwab actually wanted to know. Curtis probably had few opportunities to talk to anyone from offplanet.

". . . and then, there's the hotel. Nobody calls it anything but the hotel. I suppose it's got a name written down somewhere, but I don't know it. No one ever bothered to put up a sign." Curtis grinned and glanced at Schwab. "With only one, who needs names, right? It's the center of everything. Governor Morris has his office there. Cowdin—he's in charge of our mining operation here, as well as the Parians; that is, if anyone's in charge of the Parians. They just seem to do what they want no matter what we have in mind. Fortunately, what we want seems to be about the same thing they do. Anyway, Cowdin has an office in the hotel, but he had another one built outside the field to be closer to the center of his operations. You won't have any trouble finding whoever sent for you. It's all right there in one building. Bar on the ground floor. Good place to wait. Sooner or later, everyone comes through the bar. They get more business done there than in their offices."

The dustrover continued its floating journey over the bumpy terrain, eventually penetrating the static field around the concession—a minimum Earth environment field, designed to keep dust clouds out of the human colony and stabilize the temperature within. Other than slightly cleaner air and a minute drop in temperature, Schwab noticed little difference. Curtis, enjoying himself, pointed out the various sights of interest: a warehouse, another warehouse, an ore storage depot.

". . . and those elms—Morris's folly, we call them. Governor Morris had them brought from Earth to make us feel at home."

The elms, evidently imported as saplings, all looked as though they needed water. They stood at regular intervals along the sides of the warehouses, leaves drooping and tinted a peculiar shade of green.

"They look sick."

"It's the light," answered Curtis. "Something in the upper atmosphere. It makes everything look sick on this planet. Look at my face. Believe it or not, in Earth-normal lighting I've got a tan."

Schwab looked at the man's washed-out face, then at the backs of his own hands. Even the freckles looked faded and bland. "I see what you mean."

The dustrover pulled up in front of a five-story building with a wide, synthetic wood porch like something from Schwab's Iowa boyhood. He smiled faintly at the incongruous image; Iowa transplanted 75 million kilometers from Earth. Probably some psychologist had designed the hotel to make the colonists feel at home. Or, alternatively, someone from Iowa.

Schwab shook hands with Curtis again and jumped out of the dustrover. He pulled the planet bag out of the backseat and settled it onto his shoulder, feeling the full 25 kilo weight.

As he reached the first step on the hotel porch, Curtis called after him: "Ernie, if you have any problems, remember, I'm around."

"What kind of problems?"

Curtis shrugged. "Who knows? Anything. Finding the guy who sent for you, or something like that. In any case, if you do have any problems, let me know."

Schwab nodded, then waved with his free hand. He carried the bag up the steps and through the open door of the hotel, dropping it with a muffled thud when he reached the check-in desk.

A young man sat behind the desk, his attention focused on a magazine viewer. He glanced up briefly, then returned his gaze to the viewer. Schwab could see shapes moving on the viewscreen and hear a tiny voice from the speaker discussing a recent election on Earth.

Schwab cleared his throat several times.

The man continued to watch the viewer.

Finally, losing patience, Schwab leaned across the counter. "Are you in charge here?"

The man answered without looking up. "Yep."

"Then you can help me, can't you?"

"Depends on what you want."

"A room."

"Full up."

"Since there's only one hotel, that means I have to sleep outside."

"Guess so."

"Tell me something. Are you employed by Diversicorp?"

"Nope. Work for my uncle."

"Can I talk to him?"

"Sure, when he gets back."

"When will that be?"

"Sometime this week."

"When he gets back, tell him Mr. Schwab—"

The man looked up. "Oh, you're Schwab. You're the reason we're full up. You've been booked into the last room."

Reluctantly, the desk clerk pushed the hold button on the viewer and stood up. He checked Schwab in and led him upstairs to his room, a corner room overlooking what Curtis had called "the street." The room was adequate for his needs and also convenient to the Diversicorp offices. Schwab had no intention of growing roots on Paria. He wondered, briefly, whether anything—even the elms—could grow roots on Paria.

Sometime between checking in and going upstairs, a sudden and—at least to Schwab—unexpected rain began pounding on the hotel, the static field too weak to repel the heavy drops. From his window, Schwab could see puddles quickly forming in the ruts on the street. Usually, rain cleared the air. On Paria, it seemed to have little effect.

Rain began to bead on the window. Schwab sat down in a chair, watching the street and trying to think of how to make his presence known. He decided to take Curtis's advice and go downstairs to the bar. If the bartender was more helpful than the desk clerk, maybe he would be able to tell him where to get a lead on whoever wanted to see him.

As abruptly as it had begun, the Parian rain stopped. Outside the window, the dingy sun steamed the flatlands. In the distance, Schwab could make out the native Parian mounds. He could even see specks emerging from the tops of them, Parians beginning to rebuild the mounds after the rain.

He stood and paced in the hotel room, debating again between the bar and the Diversicorp office. Inexplicably, he had a sensation of being watched, of not being alone in the room. He looked around, checked the bathroom and closet. All were empty, yet the feeling persisted. He looked out the window at the empty street, momentarily expecting to find someone watching him from the doorway of the warehouse across the street. He found no one. He decided to check the hall and walked to the door.

The hall, too, proved to be empty. He started down the hall to the stairs, planning to go down to the bar and let a few stiff drinks rid him of his malaise. A partially open doorway down the corridor caught his attention. He walked toward it, wondering if someone was behind the door. He reached it and stood outside a moment, looking into the office. A man lay inside on a couch, head against one arm of the couch, forearm wearily resting on his brow as though momentarily trying to block out the light.

From Schwab's position, only the top of the man's head and one arm were exposed over the end of the couch. The office itself was book-lined and cluttered. A desk near the couch was stacked with folders. Almost impulsively, without having any idea why he was doing it, Schwab stepped into the room, walking quietly to the end of the couch. He stopped behind the man and bent forward slightly. Still unaware of Schwab's presence, perhaps dozing, the man continued to lie on the couch, breathing regularly.

At that moment, Schwab felt himself reach out—not physically; the Ernest Schwab at the end of the couch continued to stand motionless over the reclining figure—toward the man with his mind. He felt, distinctly, a moment of contact, mind to mind, then an overwhelming rush of data from the other mind: emotions, thoughts, memories—most of all, memories. Somehow, he knew the man was Jeremy Morris, governor of the Earth colony on Paria. He knew he was in Morris's mind, following the man's life back through the years of college, secondary and elementary school, back to the earliest moments of Morris's childhood and at last to what seemed like a few moments of warm security. The information, everything Morris had been or done, hurtled past in unbelievable complexity, yet at the same time in utter clarity. Schwab was simultaneously aware of the rush of the collapsed years through his mind and the few seconds it took to occur, the blinding intensity of the images from Morris's mind and the dull reality of the office around them. Mentally, he struggled, trying futilely to break contact, to separate his mind from the mind of the man on the couch. The effort had no effect. The images and sensations still rushed past.

In another part of his own mind, Schwab knew what was happening. He knew Morris's mind was being emptied, cleared of its every memory—that Morris would be nothing but an empty shell, a husk, shucked and abandoned. He knew he was responsible for what was happening as surely as if he had willed it. Yet, try—strain against the flow of memory—as he would, he could do nothing to halt it.

Abruptly, the cascading impressions of Morris's past life ended. Schwab's mind felt contact beginning to break. His mind filled with a name, clearly pronounced and at least three times as strong as the other impressions from Morris's mind—*Regina!*

CHAPTER 2

The contact broke. As neatly and precisely as a door closing, Schwab felt himself cut off from Morris's mind. At the same time, he felt himself repossess his own mind and body. Momentarily, he felt as though he were about to faint. His legs were weak and rubbery, his stomach nauseous. He had to strain to keep from losing control of his bowels. He stumbled toward the door, almost tripped and caught himself with the flat of his hand against the wall. He took two or three deep breaths, shaking his head in an effort to clear it. It swirled with confusing images. He had heard of mindwipes, the aberrant telepathic capacity to destroy another man's mind. He knew he had just committed one. But how?

Schwab pushed himself away from the wall and looked at the man on the couch. To Schwab, the last few seconds had been a tumult of events, a lifetime compressed to an instant. Yet Morris, his arm still resting on his forehead, looked utterly unchanged. In spite of Schwab's intellectual conviction to the contrary, he felt himself begin to hope. Perhaps the few instants had not actually mindwiped Morris. Perhaps the entire event had occurred only in Schwab's own mind. He started toward the man on the couch.

"Governor Morris?"

The man remained motionless.

Schwab reached out and shook him gently. "Governor."

The arm fell away from the forehead. One look at Morris's face, twisted and contorted, told Schwab all he needed to know. His hopes faded. Morris's mind had been emptied.

Schwab turned from the empty shell on the couch. His first impulse was to flee, to leave the hotel and the colony without looking back. On Earth, or on any of the densely populated planets, he might have a chance. A man determined enough could always lose himself. On Paria, a colony world with a population only slightly larger than the *Chanticleer*'s crew, he would have no chance at all. Without help. . . .

Schwab hesitated and glanced around the office. He could think of only one source of help. Carefully, he closed the door into the hall and went over to Morris's desk. He touched on the phone and obtained Curly Curtis's number from the directory computer; he punched out the number on the keyboard.

Curly's face appeared on the screen and he answered almost immediately. "Ernie, hi. What's up?"

"I need some help."

"Sure. What can I do for you?"

"I have to get off Paria."

"The crew you came down with left about ten minutes ago. I don't have any idea when the next one's scheduled. Ernie, you look sick. What—"

"I am sick, but that's not the reason I'm leaving. I just. . . ." Schwab hesitated, uncertain whether to tell Curly on the phone. "I'll tell you about it when I see you. But do me a favor. Don't tell anyone I'm leaving, or even that you talked to me. As far as you know, you just dropped me at the hotel and haven't seen me since."

"Ernie, what's going on?"

"I don't know yet. I need something else from you, too."

"Shoot."

"A place to hide."

Curly looked incredulous. "*Hide!* What do you mean,

hide? You can't hide around here. This place is too small. And why do you want to?"

"I'll explain when I see you. Where can we meet?"

Curly thought a moment, then gave Schwab instructions on how to reach a nearby warehouse. "You probably won't see anyone there. We've shipped out most of the ore containers. If you do see anyone, just show them your Diversicorp ID and tell them I cleared you."

"Fine. I'll see you in half an hour."

Schwab touched the phone off and glanced at Morris. The twisted face had lost some of its sharp look of pain. The muscles were settling back into place. He tried and failed to think of anything he could do for Morris. He could only leave and hope Morris would remain undiscovered until after he left Paria.

Schwab rose from the desk and walked to the door, cautiously at first to avoid any return of the nausea and dizziness. He opened the door and glanced into the corridor. Somehow, he expected it to be filled with people, the colony's security guards and spectators. It was empty. When he was sure he had regained complete control of himself, he entered the corridor. As the emotionally drained feeling began to lessen, he started back toward his room, planning to pick up his planet bag.

He stopped at the head of the stairs. If he left the hotel carrying the bag, the desk clerk would be suspicious. He would have to sacrifice the bag and his belongings. He started downstairs, wondering what he would do if the desk clerk decided to engage him in conversation before he made it to the front door.

On the ground floor, he started across the lobby. The desk clerk, still absorbed in his magazine viewer, took only perfunctory notice at first, then seemed to sit up straight.

"Mr. Schwab."

Schwab stopped, his back to the desk, not trusting himself to turn around. "What?"

"There's a message here for you."

Message? Schwab turned and approached the desk, forcing himself to react normally.

The desk clerk handed him a phonefaxed sheet of paper. Schwab looked it over. The original had been on Diversicorp stationery. It explained briefly and succinctly that a mistake had occurred. Schwab was no longer needed on Paria. He could return to the *Chanticleer* on the next shuttle.

Schwab examined both sides of the paper. Like the order that had originally brought him to the surface, it carried no indication of its point of origin. In spite of that, it did provide one thing Schwab needed, an excuse for taking his belongings with him.

Schwab shook his head and summoned a look of disgust. "Did you see this thing? I wish these people would make up their minds. First they want me down here, then they don't." Schwab shrugged. "I suppose one of these days they'll get coordinated."

The desk clerk made appropriately sympathetic noises, before insisting he would still have to charge Schwab for a full day.

Schwab agreed and went back upstairs. It had taken all his willpower to carry on a normal conversation. He found himself sweating profusely. Still, the order gave him a legitimate excuse to leave the hotel. At any moment, he expected someone to find Morris. The cry would go up. With Schwab's orderly and explained departure, the desk clerk might not immediately think of him when the authorities began checking.

Schwab carried the planet bag downstairs. He paused at the desk long enough to initial the computer-printed bill, then heaved the bag to his shoulder and went outside. The sun had already dried most of the ground, leaving only occasional trickles of water in the bottom of wheel ruts. Schwab headed for the main street and strode to the warehouse Curly had described. Twice, dustrovers—their gigantic wheels now caked with mud—lumbered past. The drivers barely glanced at him.

In the entranceway to the warehouse, Schwab lowered the bag to the ground and tried the door. Unlocked. He moved the bag inside and looked around for a sign of Curly. Seeing none he called out once. His voice echoed in the enormous empty building.

Schwab waited just inside the door. As he waited, his nervousness increased. When he had just about decided to go outside and look for Curly, the door opened, briefly silhouetting Curly's bulky frame.

"Where have you—"

"Sorry, Ernie, but all hell broke loose out there." Curly looked at Schwab. "I think you know what I'm talking about."

"Governor Morris."

Curly nodded.

"Look, Curly, you're going to have to trust me."

"What happened?"

"I don't know. But you'll have to believe I didn't intentionally do anything. If you don't want to help me, I'll understand, but—"

"Tell me about it, Ernie."

Schwab told him all he knew. Curly listened, occasionally glancing up at Schwab as though trying to weigh the truth of what he heard. When Schwab finished, Curly kept looking at him. Schwab shrugged. "That's it."

"You're sure."

"Positive. I don't know anything else. I don't know why. I don't know how. I did it. That's all I know."

Curly considered Schwab a moment longer, then nodded. "Okay, Ernie, follow me."

Schwab picked up his bag and followed Curly to the

other side of the warehouse. Curly took out a set of keys, pressed one to the lock and waited for the door to slide back. The light in the room—evidently an office—came on automatically.

"You'll probably be safe here. We only use this office when there's activity in the warehouse. Stay here. I'll go out and see what's happening. The last I heard nobody knew anything. They'd found Morris and that was it. I'll be back as soon as I can. If it's possible, we'll get you on the next shuttle to the *Chanticleer*."

Curly turned and started for the door

"Curly."

The man stopped and glanced around, answering Schwab's question before it was asked. "Because I worked with you a long time, Ernie, I believe you. If I'm wrong—" he shrugged "—at least I did the right thing. Friends are hard to come by."

"You're not wrong, Curly."

Something—doubt?—flickered behind Curly's eyes. "I hope not."

Curly left.

Schwab spent an anxious half hour in the warehouse office. He tried to think, to piece together the situation and his role. He knew too little to make sense of the events. They had happened. He had participated in them. Beyond that, they could have happened to a complete stranger.

Only one fact seemed clear. Whoever had ordered him to the surface, then rescinded the order—both actions done anonymously—would be involved. The two events—the call to the surface and Morris's mindwiping—could not be coincidence. But why had the person responsible chosen Schwab? And how had he accomplished the mindwiping?

Another possibility, less acceptable and more upsetting, occurred to Schwab Perhaps the call to the surface had in fact been coincidence. Perhaps Schwab himself was totally responsible for the mindwiping, involuntarily reducing Morris to a shell. He would not know until he had contacted the person behind his orders. If it turned out something uncontrollable in Schwab had committed the mindwiping—what then?

Schwab put aside the thought. Little could be gained from speculation without facts.

Curly Curtis returned a half hour later bringing news and a sandwich.

Schwab, realizing he had eaten nothing since the last meal call on the *Chanticleer*, wolfed down the sandwich, listening to Curly.

Curly described the confusion at the hotel. Morris's secretary had come into the office with a stack of papers for his signature. She had assumed Morris was sleeping. Knowing the hours her boss kept and his obvious need for sleep, she had left the papers and returned to her other duties. Finally, a call had come through from the Diversicorp mining operations director. She tried to put the call through. Morris failed to respond. She went into the office. She tried to awaken Morris. She became frantic and called the concession doctor. The doctor had never seen a victim of mindwiping. His diagnosis took more time. When Morris's condition had finally become clear, pandemonium broke loose. At that point, Curly had arrived at the hotel. Security guards were running in several directions at once.

Schwab finished the last of the sandwich and looked at Curly. "What about me?"

Curly shook his head. "Don't worry about it. They haven't even begun to think about you yet. But they will. We have to get you out of here."

"And go where?"

"Offplanet. Out of sight, out of mind."

Schwab knew Curly was right. If he remained on Paria, the only stranger in the colony, attention would focus on him. If he reached the *Chanticleer*, he would have the one thing he needed—time. With time, he might be able to do more for himself than run.

Schwab took the phonefax order canceling his original call and handed it to Curly. "I was handed this just before I left the hotel. It gives me a legitimate reason for leaving."

Curly read the order, frowning. "Who sent this?"

"I don't know. My original orders didn't have an authorization either."

"It could have been anyone." Curly looked up and grinned. "Even me. Everyone has access to the central Com Room."

"But it's on Diversicorp stationery. That should narrow it down some."

"Not on Paria. If someone wanted Diversicorp stationery to cut false orders, he would have very little problem obtaining it. And there's another problem."

"What?"

"Ernie, I'm taking everything you've told me on faith. I'm basing my assumptions on your information. If we assume this order has something to do with Morris—"

"It *has* to."

"Okay. Whoever sent it wanted you down here. Now—" Curly shook the phonefax paper "—they want you off the surface, or at least trying to get off. If you use these orders, I'll lay you ten to one you'll be in custody before the hour's out."

"What's the alternative?"

"I can get you on an ore shuttle. They're not as comfortable as passenger shuttles, but you'll survive."

"Okay, let's go."

They left the warehouse and started away from the direction of the shuttleport. Schwab noticed the direction and called it to Curly's attention.

"We have to get a dustrover, Ernie. No one walks

around here. By walking, you just call attention to yourself."

They passed two warehouses and turned into a motorpool area for Diversicorp. Curly checked out a dustrover, picked up Schwab at the entrance and headed for the shuttleport.

"Ernie, tell me something."

"Sure."

"What are you going to do once you're offplanet?"

"What do you mean?"

"You can't just let the whole thing drop. If it's swept under the rug, there'll still be someone out there who's responsible but getting off scot-free."

"*If* someone else is responsible. Somehow, I may have done it."

"I doubt that."

"Why do you doubt it? It's as likely an explanation as any."

"I know you."

"I appreciate your confidence, Curly, but do any of us really know anyone else? Do the mothers who raise children to become mass murderers really know their children?"

"Most of the children they raise don't sit around worrying about things like that. You're worrying about it. I think that makes some kind of difference."

"I hope so."

When they reached the shuttle landing area, Curly parked the dustrover. No one paid any attention to them, so, following Curly, Schwab carried his planet bag to the nearest shuttle.

The shuttles, totally automatic, were designed like flatbed trucks, the long center sections merely a framework of struts and girders. Once they were positioned in the center section, the giant ore containers themselves, filled on Paria between freighter visits, provided the outer hull of the ships. The aft section contained the engines. The forward section contained cramped quarters for two men, thought of by the designers as backup systems for the automatic equipment.

Curly led Schwab to the forward section When Schwab climbed through the awkward entrance port, Curly stood on the ground and passed up the planet bag.

"Just stay inside until lift-off, Ernie. That should be in about—" Curly glanced at his watch "—15 minutes."

Schwab looked at Curly's upturned face, his own expression pleading. "Curly, am I doing the right thing?"

"Of course you're doing the right thing. What else can you do?"

"Go back."

"Go back! Why?"

"I have to find out who sent those orders. Either way— if it's perfectly innocent or if it means something—I'll have a better idea what's going on."

"Ernie, don't be stupid. You're safe here. Once you're on the *Chanticleer*, you'll be safer. Give things a chance to die down. I saw those people at the hotel. They're excited. If they come after you now, there's no telling what they'll do. Morris was well liked around here by most people. Let them cool off. Then you can make inquiries. Then you can try and do something. But now—"

"If I wait, it may be too late. If there is any connection between my orders and Morris, any evidence of it may disappear. If I leave, I may never get a chance to clear myself."

"Let people calm down, Ernie."

Schwab made up his mind. If he left Paria, he might leave his only chance to learn the truth, even if that truth were something about himself. He climbed down through the shuttleport and dropped to the ground. The more he ought about his decision, the more certain he was that his choice had been correct. Paria held all the answers; the *Chanticleer* none.

Schwab walked toward the dustrover. "Take me back to the hotel, Curly."

Curly fell into step beside him. "You're making a mistake, Ernie. I can feel it."

"Curly, I can't just sit back and let things happen to me. I have to do something."

"I still say it's a mistake."

CHAPTER 3

Curly dropped Schwab near the hotel. They made arrangements to meet at the shuttleport two hours later. Schwab stood for a moment outside the hotel. Beyond trying to look inconspicuous and finding whoever authorized his orders, he had no plan. Though Curly had said anyone might have access to Diversicorp stationery, Schwab decided to check the company's ground personnel first. The best place to begin the task was in the hotel. He started up the steps.

As soon as he stepped into the lobby, Schwab knew Curly had been right. He had made a mistake. He had hoped to enter the hotel with the initial confusion over Morris's mindwiping still in progress. He hoped the confusion would allow him to make inquiries. Instead, suspicion had already narrowed to him. Two men—colony security guards—stood at the desk, their backs to Schwab, questioning the desk clerk. Schwab heard his name being spoken. He felt himself begin to panic. If they had already narrowed the investigation to him, he had no hope of moving freely in the colony. He had no hope at all of saving himself. He stood just inside the door, rooted to the floor, trying to think of an alternative to fleeing.

The desk clerk's eyes wandered past the security guard's face and over the man's shoulder. He saw Schwab, blinked once and started to point.

Schwab bolted, somehow managing to open the front door of the hotel and get out onto the dusty street. He looked both ways, hoping to see Curly, but there was no sign of his friend. He looked out at the Parian mounds. A line on the ground about 100 meters from the nearest mound marked the static field that kept the Parian dirt from blowing through the colony area. Dust devils swirled against the static field like powdery beasts trying to butt their way into the Earthmen's sanctuary.

Schwab took a deep breath. He knew he had only one choice. With the colony alerted, security guards already looking for him, he could do nothing else. Though what happened to Morris had nothing to do with Schwab's free will, he had no doubt he would be held responsible for it and sent to a criminal rehabilitation center to have his own personality blotted from existence. It would not matter to them how he had done it, nor why. They would see only that he was responsible. He felt a new compulsion seize him, a compulsion born of fear.

He turned toward the nearest Parian mound and ran: down the long colony street, through the static field around the concession, across the expanse of ground between the human enclave and the mound. Sudden swirls of dust sprang up and subsided around him. Dust filled his eyes and covered his skin. Expecting to be shot down any second, he increased his pace, chest heaving, arms and legs pumping.

He reached the base of the nearest mound and began scrambling up the side, his boots slipping in the loose dirt. He had seen no Parians as he approached. At close range, the mounds were taller than he expected, somewhere between ten and 15 meters from base to crest, becoming steeper and narrower toward the top. At one point, he almost lost his footing completely and had to scramble on all fours to regain his balance.

Near the top of the mound, he slowed to catch his breath and glanced back. A concession security guard—one of the men he had seen in the hotel—loped after him, just crossing the line drawn in the dirt by the static field.

Schwab looked away from the man and crawled the last few meters to the crest of the mound. On the other side, the mound sloped down again forming a gigantic cone of dirt, like the belly of a small volcano. The funnel of the cone dropped down at least 30 meters before it became lost in the blackness of the Parian diggings below. He glanced back once at the security guard—now nearing the base of the mound and shouting. Schwab looked back at the cone. He had little choice. Without thinking, he jumped.

Schwab tumbled and rolled down the inside of the mound, dropping the 30 meters like a man falling down a snowy slope, a trail of dirt billowing up behind him, the dark hole at the center of the funnel growing below him. At last, after what seemed an eternity, the dark hole swallowed him.

He fell a few meters in darkness.

Abruptly, he landed, knees buckling under him, air exploding from his lungs. Exhausted, he lay crumpled on the floor of the tunnel, the wind knocked from him. He gave himself a cursory examination for any serious wounds, found none and managed to get to his feet. Staring in both directions along the tunnel, his eyes slowly began to adjust to the dim light. On either side, the tunnel was the same, dimly lit with occasional brighter spots of light on the floors, other openings to the surface.

Bewildered and lost already, with no idea where any tunnel would lead, he picked a direction at random and started to run. His legs felt sore; each step added to the pain. Vaguely, some place in the back of his mind, Schwab realized he was thinking like a child, irrationally seeking security from a fearful world. He desperately wanted to be alone and think out what he would do. At the same time, he recognized that there might be nothing to think out. Could some genetic defect within him push him into conduct he would never rationally choose for himself?

He ran through the gray tunnel world, making random choices when he came to tunnel intersections. In the poor light and unfamiliar tunnels, he felt as though he had run for kilometers. Each tunnel was as gray and lacking in distinctive character as the last. He had no way of telling whether he had run in a straight line or in circles.

Finally, unable to continue, he stopped, panting, leaning on his knees to catch his breath. He squatted in the tunnel, trying to work out his next move. When his breath finally stopped rasping in his chest and his pulse stopped pounding at his temples, he began to be aware of the tunnels again. He heard the first of the scraping sounds.

Almost instinctively, he knew what was causing the sounds. The Parians were aware of an intruder in their tunnels. He tried to pinpoint the source of the noises. They could have come from any direction. No matter where he turned, no matter which way he ran, he might meet the Parians.

The noises grew louder. Even if he chose the right direction—assuming there was a right direction—he could only hope to evade the creatures for a short time. They knew their tunnels. He did not. He stood up and listened.

His feeling of bewilderment intensified, as simultaneously, he wanted both to run and to stay. Either way, he would be caught. What would the Parians do to an interloper in their tunnels? He knew nothing about the native creatures of Paria. He knew only what men would do in the same situation. The thought chilled him.

Schwab started back along the tunnel, uncertain whether he was breaking new ground or retracing his steps. He turned into a side tunnel. The noises grew louder. He retreated to the intersection. Above him, a light and air hole let dull sunlight shine on him. He looked at his clothes, frosted with dust. He ran his hand over his forehead and felt the sweat-caked grime. The saliva in his mouth tasted thick and dirty. He wanted someone to come and rescue him, take him away from the horror and confusion.

The scraping sounds drew nearer.

A rancid odor rose in the tunnels, signalling the Parians' approach. Schwab looked at the tunnel floor, and in the dirt under the air hole, he saw the footprint. At that moment, any hope he had of escaping the tunnels and the Parians died. The footprint meant he had failed to recognize a spot he had passed before—how many times? If he could not differentiate new tunnels from old, he had no hope of escaping the maze. Any further flight futile, he stood there, the light casting a dull glow around his feet and the footprint that condemned him.

The scrapings increased. The first of the rat-bodied creatures emerged from a side tunnel, followed by others from every tunnel. Each of the creatures was twice the size of a large dog. They moved with scraping, shuffling steps, their great bodies swinging from side to side.

Schwab backed against the tunnel wall. The smell was almost intolerable. It reminded him of sewers. Irrationally, he kept thinking the Parians planned to eat him. At the same time, he knew they would not eat him. They could never metabolize him, any more than he could digest a rock. They had evolved on Paria, while he was a product of Earth evolution.

Just as he convinced himself he would probably not be eaten, simply torn apart as an intruder, he heard a vaguely human voice calling his name.

"Mr. Schwab, it is futile to run farther. You cannot escape."

At first, he thought one of the Parians had spoken. Finally, he realized the unlikelihood of that explanation. Though the Parians must have had some way of communicating with each other and with the humans who gave them tools in exchange for ore, the possibility of their being capable of mimicking human speech was low.

At that point, he saw officer Daniels, the security guard from the hotel. Daniels emerged from a side tunnel, saw Schwab and started toward him.

"Ah, there you are," said Daniels, as though he had been waiting all afternoon to have lunch with Schwab. He approached and extended his arm, gesturing for Schwab to take a coin-sized disk in his hand. "You're under arrest, Mr. Schwab. This disk—take it."

Schwab, his brain still numb from fear and exertion, took the disk.

"It will explain your rights," said Daniels. "Press it."

Schwab pressed the disk. The voice from the disk, clear and echoing in the tunnels, began telling Schwab his rights. Though it informed him of his right to remain silent, Schwab felt he had little use for the information. At that point, he could hardly think, much less speak.

Daniels pointed down one of the tunnels in the direction he had come and told Schwab to follow. Some Parians, evidently helping Daniels, followed Schwab.

In spite of their slow pace, the walk back seemed quicker than Schwab's initial route. They emerged from the tunnels at a man-made excavation near a squat plastone building, evidently the mining operations building for Diversicorp. The Parians remained behind. As they came out onto the plain, Daniels pulled a stunclub from a sheath on his hip, turned it up to high and flicked it on. The tip lit. He cautioned Schwab against doing anything foolish. They started for the concession.

Schwab's head began to clear. The full impact of the mistake he had made—his return—came home to him. Curly had been right. At least in the *Chanticleer*, Schwab would have had time to think out a coherent plan. In custody, Schwab would have little hope of doing anything.

THE following two weeks were a blur in Schwab's memory. Paria, too small a human settlement to have its own criminal justice system, had to hold any prisoners until a federation ship came into the area for transporting the prisoner back to Earth. Schwab's "cell" was the same hotel room he had initially rented, now guarded by four men. Once, an official of some sort with a voicewriter tried to interrogate him. He relied on the information on the disk Daniels had given him, declining to talk to anyone until he had consulted a lawyer.

His only unofficial visitor, Curly Curtis, showed up on the second day.

Curly walked into the room already shaking his head. "Ernie, I told you—"

"I know. I know." Schwab waved him into silence. "That's all behind us now, Curly. The question is what happens next."

"Do you have any money saved?"

"Some. Why?"

"You'll need a lawyer."

"I don't know any lawyers."

"I know one. His name's E. W. Benson. He helped me out of that—ah—scrap I was in on Earth."

Schwab remembered. With a month of planetside leave coming, Curly had set up housekeeping with a girl. Her husband had disapproved. He tried to break her contract with a large club instead of legal action. Curly had defended the girl and himself, landing in jail for his trouble.

Schwab thought it over and nodded. "Okay, talk to him and see if he'll take the case. Talk to him as soon as you can. I already feel it closing in."

Curly looked momentarily confused. "Feel what closing in?"

"The system. I'm afraid of it. Once the wheels start rolling, I won't be able to do anything to stop them. I need help. I don't even have the faintest idea what really happened. And they won't care. I'd appreciate it if you would talk to this—what was his name?"

"Benson. I already talked to him. As soon as they get you to Earth, he'll see you. By the way, the *Chanticleer* left this morning."

Gene. Schwab smiled and shook his head. The *Chanticleer* had left him behind.

"Curly."

"What?"

"Did they get the starboard debris sensors fixed?"

A FEDERATION cruiser arrived in orbit around Paria at the end of Schwab's second week in custody. Under heavy guard, he was transferred to the ship. Once aboard, he was locked in a high security cabin for the trip to Earth. No one spoke to him. No one interrogated him. Someone brought his meals to his cabin and left without a word.

An identical procedure was followed at the Earth end of the journey: Schwab was quickly escorted to the surface by silent guards. At a maximum security facility near Los Angeles, he was photographed, voiceprinted, fingerprinted and genotyped, then led to an isolation cell. From that point on, he saw no one until the lawyer, Benson, arrived.

REGINA

I lie on my couch. The computers on the wall opposite me are blank and lifeless, unused since the man Schwab's arrival. When they are on, the colored lights reflect in the blown glass figurines of my animals, the cuddliest animals from a dozen worlds. They sit on top of the console and the memory banks. I love my figurines. In many ways, I often think, they are my only reason for being—to collect them, to have them, to love them. Without moving my head, I can see glass fawns from Earth, glass ernews from Wolff-74-5, glass veltors from the distant world circling Alpha Centauri. Each of the creatures looks friendly, kind and helpful, unlike men.

CHAPTER 4

Benson stepped through the scanner at security post seven. The guard nodded and opened the inside door. Benson walked down the long corridor, past the prison facility's administration offices and stopped at the final scanner station before entering the prison proper. He had already gone through four previous scannings between the parking area and the inside. He would have to repeat the process on his way out. The federation maximum security holding facility took few chances. Everyone, lawyers included, took the same route, which was, in Benson's opinion, time-wasting and tedious.

He stopped at the block warden's office long enough to find out Schwab's cell number. A guard carrying a stunclub led him the short distance to the cell. After Curly Curtis's call two weeks before, Benson had found himself looking forward to his first meeting with Schwab. He had never represented a telepath. The experience promised to be interesting.

Just that morning, Benson had gone over Schwab's psychological profile. The man appeared to be of normal intelligence, a career starship hand; he was born and raised on Earth but had spent most of his adult life in space. He was said to be good at his job and well liked. Nothing in the profile suggested more than acceptable variations in his personality. Only one quality—telepathy—separated him from the rest of humanity. According to the psy-rating on his profile, Schwab was a low-grade receptor telepath, capable of sensing accurately other people's thoughts under proper conditions—occasionally capable of picking up the thoughts directly—but unable to give a consistent performance. One fact continued to argue against the profile's accuracy: the charge against Schwab—criminal telepathy.

Benson and the guard arrived at Schwab's cell. The guard touched his master key to the plate by the cell door. The door slid open.

"You have half an hour, Mr. Benson."

"Thank you."

Benson entered the cell. The door closed behind. In front of him, Schwab, preparing to eat his noon meal, looked up from the table. Benson introduced himself and told Schwab to go ahead and eat.

Schwab stripped away the wrapping from the main course. Steam rose from the roast beef. He glanced up at Benson, his voice even and controlled. "You know what I hate most about this place, Mr. Benson?"

"Being caged up?"

"No. You expect that. It's the details. Everywhere I look something reminds me I'm in jail. If they had just thrown me in a big stone cell, clanged shut the door and walked away with their keys jingling on a ring, I would have gotten the message. But *this* place—everywhere I look they repeat the message. They've thought of everything. Watch this."

Schwab picked a fork off the plate, held out his forearm and tried to drive the fork into the muscle. The fork touched the skin and crumbled.

Schwab brushed the plastic shards from his arm and looked up. "I couldn't even kill myself to get out of here."

"Do you want to kill yourself?"

"I don't even have the *choice*. That's what bothers me." Schwab tugged at the front of his light-blue prison pullover, the number "7246" in white above the pocket. "And these things fall apart like mildewed potato sacks if I don't put them on within two minutes after opening the package. They don't want me to hang myself." Schwab gestured around at the small cell. "But from *what*?"

Benson looked around at the bare walls and ceiling. Schwab's psychological profile was questionable on the point of his telepathic capability. Perhaps it had been wrong about the man's basic stability. Benson decided to pursue the subject a moment, hoping to learn more about Schwab. "If you had the choice, would you commit suicide?"

"Are you kidding? It's having the choice that bothers me. It was merely an example. The point is I don't have any choices in here. Besides, I've got a better way out of here than hanging myself."

"What?"

"You."

Benson smiled, a noncommittal and reassuring smile. He sat down on the cot opposite Schwab. How often had he heard that same thought expressed? How often, in spite of his client's confidence, had the truth run counter to expectations? "I'm not a miracle worker, Mr. Schwab. I'm just a lawyer. I'll make sure your rights are protected, but I can't change the facts."

"I don't want the facts changed. I just want out. I didn't do any of the things they said. I want you to show them that—you and that machine of theirs."

"The kineticorder?"

"That's right. If it does what they say it does, I don't have anything to worry about. It will show them I'm innocent."

Benson had encountered too many misconceptions about the kineticorder to trust Schwab's evaluation of his situation. "What do they say it does?"

"Reveals the truth. It scans your mind and produces a picture of the important events."

"First of all, the kineticorder can't reveal the absolute truth. I wish it could. It would put me out of business, but society would be better off."

"Okay, so they probe your mind and get your version of the event." Schwab waved his hand in a dismissing gesture. "Same thing. They'll know I never intended to do anything to Morris. The whole time, I felt. . . ." Schwab hesitated, then glanced around at the cell. "I felt like I do here, as though I had no free will at all. With their machine, they'll see that. They'll be inside my mind and know I'm not guilty. For God's sake, I don't feel guilty. Don't I have to intend to commit this crime to be guilty of it—I mean, if I accidentally kill someone with my car, that's different than intentionally running him down, isn't it?"

Benson nodded. "Yes, there's an element of intent in the basic definition of criminal telepathy. Your mistake is thinking the kineticorder will show that intent. It doesn't. It can't. It doesn't scan your mind."

"I've read that—"

"I don't care what you've read. The kineticorder scans your body, not your mind. The computer integrates and correlates all the information taken from all the witnesses, along with a scan of the locale. It presents a complete and objective picture of your actions—and only your actions—not what's in your mind. Legally, kineticorder evidence is considered as a conclusive presumption of fact. That means any evidence we might have that contradicts it will never get into court. It's considered better evidence than eye-witness testimony. People make mistakes. The kineticorder doesn't. Memory fades, but your body remembers—in the sense that it is altered by everything, every experience it goes through from birth to death."

Thoughtful, Schwab returned to his meal. "It doesn't probe your mind?"

"No. As I said, the scan just records an objective account of your actions during the relevant time."

"Isn't that circumstantial evidence?"

Benson, watching Schwab wolf down his food, began to notice his own growling stomach, evidence—objective evidence—that the cold he had carried for the prior two weeks was finally giving way. He pushed his mind back to Schwab's question. Lunch would come later. "Yes, it's circumstantial evidence, but as the saying goes, which piece of evidence are you going to believe, the word of 100 eyewitnesses that no dog passed by or the dog tracks in the dirt? The dog tracks are circumstantial evidence, but circumstantial evidence you can't fight. In your case, you were on Paria only a few hours. You had never been there before. The environment, at least within the concession, is man-made. They should be able to get a very clear scan. From it, they'll make an equally clear tape."

Schwab put down the knife and spoon, pushing aside his empty plate. He stripped off the top of a milk container, drank and lowered it, empty, to the table. He sat a moment, evidently thinking about what he had been told. The wrinkles around his eyes contradicted the boyish, freckled appearance of his face. He looked at Benson. "So they don't scan or probe your mind, just your body. Isn't that unconstitutional or something? Self-incrimination? That disk they gave me on Paria when I was arrested said I had the right to remain silent." Schwab's voice was beginning to sound angry, the response Benson had originally anticipated. "If they take a scan off me, or whatever they do, I won't be remaining silent any more than if they beat it out of me with a rubber hose."

"Your cells," said Benson, launching into the standard explanation, "or so goes the argument that upheld the use of the kineticorder in the court of last resort, can't incriminate you any more than the objective fact of your fingerprint, or a blood sample, or for that matter your face in a lineup. At one time or another, all those tests—fingerprints, blood samples and even showing a witness the accused's face—were challenged as self-incriminating and unconstitutional. None of the arguments stood up. All of them are considered objective facts. Since the kineticorder just scans the body without touching the mind, it is considered to be a tool for obtaining objective facts, like a fingerprint pad."

None of Schwab's earlier goodwill remained in his face. He looked angry and resentful. Benson had frequently noticed the reaction among his clients. He usually let them work out their feelings, then calm down.

Schwab made an impatient gesture. "I don't want to argue with you about all the legal niceties, Mr. Benson. Using that thing's unfair. I'm not going to do it. If all they take is their so-called objective evidence, I'm as good as shipped off to a rehabilitation center."

"I'm afraid you're going to have to submit to it, Mr. Schwab. If necessary, they can obtain a court order and force you."

"Physical force?"

"Yes, physical force. It makes no difference to the kineticorder's efficiency whether you go voluntarily or not.

"Okay, okay, I see that. But let me turn it around on them. You say what I'm charged with has a mental element, one they can't prove by using their machine. How *do* they prove it?"

"Inference. For example, when you spend a week obtaining a gun and setting up an ambush, then shoot someone, it is a rather simple matter to infer that you intended to bring about the person's death."

"But if they could see in my mind, instead of just the actions of my body, no one could infer I intended anything like what happened to Morris. Is that right?"

"Yes. What are you getting at?"

"I want to turn the situation around on them. You said they can't force me to submit to a mind probe, only the scan of my body, but what if I volunteer to have my mind probed? Can I get them to do it? If they do it, they'll see—"

"I've told you, Mr. Schwab, there isn't anything in use such as the kind of mind probe you're talking about. There's just the kineticorder. It's true that at one time, someone developed something like the device you want them to use. They developed it a few years before the kineticorder. They had to quit using it after the first case. With a mind probe, it really is self-incrimination."

"But if I want to incriminate myself—what then? If I want to testify, I can. Why not the same thing with a mind probe?"

"You can still testify, of course."

"If I can still testify, why can't I request a mind probe? Damn it, Mr. Benson, I may have done the act, but in here—" Schwab tapped his temple "—I'm not guilty. I don't remember any of it very clearly. I don't feel guilt about any of it. If they could read my memory or something like that, they would know I didn't do it intentionally. When I was standing outside that office, something just came over me. I didn't know who it was on the couch but I felt like I had to see him about something. I don't know what. It was like one of those dreams where you're compelled to do something, but you don't know why and at the time you don't really care. You just do it. I went into his office. I stood there in back of him for a minute. Then my mind or my thoughts—I don't know what—reached out to him and touched his mind. I don't know what it was, Mr. Benson. I don't *know*."

Schwab's hand was tense around the milk container. As he sat, looking past Benson's eyes, it crumbled.

"Go on, please," said Benson.

"If they would read my memory, they would know that. If all they read is my body, I haven't a chance in hell. I was there. The guard and the desk clerk and half the colony saw me. You don't need a computer to prove that.

In a way, I even knew what I had done. I knew I had just mindwiped Governor Morris. I'd heard about mindwipes before and I knew I'd just done one." Schwab's face was plaintive and pained. "But how, Mr. Benson, *how*?"

Gradually, Schwab became aware of the bits of plastic in his hand. He brushed them off and looked at Benson, a soft smile returning to his face. "If I get on the stand and tell them that, will it sound like your dog tracks in the dirt or the eyewitnesses?"

"I think you're right, Mr. Schwab. Whether they get the evidence because of a kineticorder scan or from witnesses it will amount to the same thing."

"Conviction."

"Not necessarily. I'm still just talking about the objective evidence. It will only make a difference in terms of reliability of the evidence. Within its limitations, a kineticorder scan is extremely reliable. Eyewitnesses never get the entire picture and their eyes sometimes play tricks on them."

"Isn't that to our advantage, trying to muddy the water as much as possible?"

"It depends on how we're going to conduct your defense. If the situation allowed more room for developing and exploiting any holes in their objective facts, I'd say we would be better off trying to avoid a kineticorder scan—the prosecution doesn't always use them. But this time, I think we might be better off with the scan."

"Why?"

"As you said, they'll get the same facts either way. This way, we'll have a 100 percent accurate record of the facts and—"

"And they'll hang me with it." Schwab shook his head. "No, Mr. Benson, I'm not going to be railroaded through the system without a fight."

"In any kind of a fight, it's better to pick your opponents' weak points."

"Like what?"

"Their strong point is that set of objective facts. Their weak point—assuming you're telling me what you feel to be the truth—is your intent. I think we should concentrate our efforts there."

"How?"

Benson smiled. "Good question. Is there anything else you can remember about that day that might help us with your defense? Anything at all."

Schwab had fallen into despondency. He shook his head, a stray wisp of hair falling across his forehead. "No, nothing. There isn't any defense, Mr. Benson. There isn't anything you can do or I can do or anyone can do. They're going to convict me with that thing and that's all there is to it."

"We don't know that yet. Try and tell me—"

Schwab's fist bounced off the table. "I've told you everything. There isn't any more. I've told you everything I know and it isn't enough. Am I supposed to start lying now? Will that help? Am I supposed to make up something to explain away what that damn machine is going to pull out of me? All I know is the truth. I can't tell them, or you, or anyone anything but that."

"The truth is enough."

"Mr. Benson, I've gone over it 100 times in my mind. I can't explain any of it. Maybe if I did lie, I could make it good enough to explain everything away. As it is, I can't do anything more than just sit here and say, ladies and gentlemen of the jury, here it is, the incriminating evidence. I'm sorry, folks, that I can't offer you more—like what it all means—but I don't even know that myself, so I guess it's up to you. And you know, Mr. Benson, what they'll do with that. I'll spend the rest of my life in a cell."

"Not the rest of your life. After rehabilitation—"

"The rest of *my* life. After rehabilitation, *I* won't exist. It'll be someone else walking around in—" Schwab tugged at the front of his pullover "—my body. And there is no way I can avoid it, is there?"

"The truth could—"

Schwab scoffed. "The truth—what is it? Do you know?"

"No, but—"

"Then where does that leave us? No, I mean, where does that leave me? Lawyers aren't sent to rehabilitation centers with their clients, are they?"

"It leaves us both on the way to finding it out."

"How?"

"First, by telling me all you can about your experience on Paria. I'll have to know as much as possible if I'm going to try and put any of it together. Second, by what we get off the kineticorder scan."

"I've already told you about Governor Morris. I've already told you about the colony. What more do you want?"

"Anything."

"There isn't any anything."

"Try. Maybe you overlooked something."

"I didn't. It's the only thing I've been thinking about for the past two weeks."

"Try again. Memory's a funny matter. If you're just going over things by yourself, sometimes you play tricks on yourself, skip important information again and again because no one's there to drag it out of you. I've done it myself. Talking it all out again—to me—might bring something out accidentally."

Schwab's face took on a pleading expression. "I swear, I've told you everything. It's all so hazy anyway. Half the time I don't even believe it actually happened. Then I look around at this damn cell and I know it happened—the colony, Morris, Regina—the whole thing."

"Who's Regina?"

Schwab looked startled. "I told you—"

Benson shook his head. "No. That's the first time you've mentioned the name. Is it some woman you were involved with?"

"No. I don't know who it is. It's just a name as far as I'm concerned. It keeps entering my mind when I go over everything. It started on Paria. After I'd done that thing to Governor Morris. . . ." Schwab, momentarily uncomfortable with the memory, inhaled deeply, calming himself. "After I'd done that to him and he didn't exist anymore, my head filled with that name, Regina, like someone was screaming it at me. Every time I remember, it comes back."

"That's all?"

"Yes. I don't know what it means. I don't know anyone named Regina. It could mean anything, even a coincidence. Maybe Governor Morris knew someone named Regina and at the instant I broke through into his mind—or whatever I did—maybe that was the name in his head and . . . and. . . ." Schwab's head shook slightly. He breathed deeply again and controlled himself. "Anyway, maybe that's how it got into my mind." Schwab stopped to think, eventually shaking his head again. "No, that doesn't exactly fit. It came at the end of that thing I did, after I had gone back through Morris's whole life and it was loud—if that's the right word for something that's just in your head—at least three times louder than Morris's other memories. Maybe it was someone important to him in his childhood or something like that."

Benson nodded, making a mental note to look into any possible connection between the name and Morris. "Maybe."

Schwab continued thinking, brow furrowed, pensive. "But the more I think about it, the more I think it had nothing at all to do with whatever was in Governor Morris's mind."

"Why?"

"Well, the name was so loud. It was completely unlike any of Morris's other memories."

"You're sure."

"I'm not sure of anything any more. I don't know what good any of this will do, Mr. Benson." Schwab managed a weak smile, some of his humor returning after the outburst of anger. "Or me."

Sitting on the cell cot, listening to Schwab and watching him, Benson decided he liked the man. More importantly, he believed him. Whether it was Schwab's demeanor, the way he told his story or even his confusion in telling it, Benson didn't know. Still, everything about it rang true.

Yet, Benson remembered other times in similar cells when he had similar feelings. How often had he sat on cell cots and believed people? How often had he been wrong? It had happened more times than Benson liked, not because he was particularly gullible—the years of law practice had removed most of his gullibility, leaving him not quite cynical but what he liked to think of as realistic— nor because all the people Benson represented were innocent. Most of them were guilty. It happened because every now and then one of his clients actually believed in his own innocence and that belief communicated itself to Benson. Legally, it made no difference what either Schwab or Benson believed. Yet, to Benson, personally and emotionally, it still mattered. He knew he could never give his best efforts to someone he believed guilty. He could give a good technical performance, true, but not a total commitment; total commitment often made the difference between an innocent man seeing prison and rehabilitation or freedom.

Benson glanced at his watch. Half past twelve. He had an appointment at 13:00 hours in his office with another client. He stood up. "I think you've given me enough to chew on for a while. I'll try to arrange a kineticorder scan as soon as possible with the prosecutor handling the case. His name's McMasters, by the way. If he tries to talk to you, you don't know anything. Tell him you won't talk without me present. Do you understand that?"

Schwab nodded. "Mr. Benson, are you sure submitting to the kineticorder scan is the right strategy?"

"Frankly, Mr. Schwab, at this point, I'm not sure of much. I'll tell you after I see it."

CHAPTER 5

Three days later, Benson found himself in the security facility's kineticorder waiting room. The same three groups of people who were always there—attorneys, guards and prisoners—stood or sat around the room. Guards predominated, most of them with stunclubs. Here and there a guard carried something with more range, a dart pistol or a sonic impacter. Considering the other safety precautions at the facility, Benson often wondered why they carried the weapons, which seemed like a potential weak link in the system, something a prisoner might be able to use in an escape attempt. But then, the Federation Penal Facility at Los Angeles had never had a successful escape. So why did the guards carry the weapons? Identity? Did they need some symbol of their authority to separate them from the prisoners?

Idle speculation. Benson had more important things to think about than the guard's self-image. One of them—possibly the most important—stood across the room, pointedly ignoring him. McMasters, the federation prosecutor in charge of Schwab's case, had been ignoring Benson for a full ten minutes. A tall, gray-haired man in his late 60s, distinguished-looking in a severe sort of way, he would have very little sympathy for Schwab. Benson had tried several cases against him and each time found him fair but hard, a man who went into court thinking it was his job to win and the system's to produce justice.

A door opened from the prison side of the waiting room. A big guard led Schwab into the room. He pointed to

Benson and the two men approached. Schwab sat in the chair next to him. The guard remained standing.

After a perfunctory greeting, Benson nodded toward McMasters. "That's the prosecutor handling your case. I'll probably see more of him than you, but you'll see enough of him."

Shifting slightly on his seat, Schwab looked at McMasters. Thoughtfully, he watched McMasters for at least 30 seconds, evidently trying to gauge the man's character by his appearance. "What kind of man is he? I can't tell much just looking at him."

The remark struck Benson as interesting. "I thought you were supposed to be telepathic."

"That's what the psychs tell me. I still can't tell much about him."

The profile had said Schwab's ability was erratic. "Mc-Masters is fair. I can at least say that about him. But he likes to win. He doesn't cut corners to do it, but he won't cut corners the other way either. He won't give you any breaks. He'll have to be convinced."

"With what?"

"Possibly with the kineticorder tape."

"But you don't really think so."

"No."

Schwab lost interest in the prosecutor and inquiring what Benson would be doing during the kineticorder scan.

"I'll be in the discovery room with McMasters, getting a sneak preview of what the jury will see. McMasters will try to get as much as he can left on the final tape. I'll try to get as much as I can thrown out. Somewhere in that process is supposed to come what the jury eventually will see, a reconstruction of what happened. After that, we'll have a separate editing session. We'll each go over the certified tapes of the other witnesses and anything else that's pertinent—oral testimony, physical evidence, that sort of thing—and finally the whole package will be presented to the jury, minus any of the melodramatic and histrionic objections they used to have in twentieth-century courtrooms. It's a much more efficient system. The jury will decide what it saw, then what they believe happened and finally what that means in terms of the law the judge will give them." Benson smiled. "And that's about it."

Schwab's weak smile surfaced again. "Yes, that's about it—for me."

Annoyed by the tone of Schwab's voice, which suggested defeat before they had even begun, Benson frowned slightly. "Listen, Schwab, we're only at the beginning of a long process. That sort of self-pitying remark doesn't do anyone any good, especially you. It just puts another obstacle in front of us. The only thing we want working against us is the prosecution, not ourselves. I want that clear right now."

Schwab nodded. The nod said he understood. It said nothing about whether he intended to take the advice. Occasionally, Benson's clients preferred to wallow in self-pity rather than contribute to their own defense. Which always added unnecessary problems to the case.

A door opened next to McMasters. A man in shirt sleeves, with a clipboard, emerged. Around the room, attorneys, recognizing him, turned their attention his way. Benson did the same.

Schwab, noticing Benson's shift of attention, looked at the man, then above him at the doorway. "What's that writing up there."

"'*Veritas Nihil Veretur Nisi Abscondi*,'" quoted Benson from memory. "It's supposed to be the motto of the place. 'The truth fears nothing but being hidden.'"

"It should be the other way around. The truth is afraid and in hiding."

The man at the door flipped through his papers, found the sheet he wanted and lifted his head, calling out into the room in a clear voice. "Schwab, Ernest J. Seven-two-four-six. This way, please."

The guard motioned for Schwab to follow the man with the clipboard. Benson followed Schwab and the guard. At the doorway, passing in front of McMasters, Benson nodded, giving a curt smile in exchange for the curt smile he received. From the man's expression, he could tell nothing about McMasters's attitude regarding the case. He would have to wait until they reached the discovery room to sound him out. He heard McMasters fall into step behind them.

They arrived at the kineticorder scanning chamber. Benson and McMasters waited outside, watching two technicians prepare Schwab. They stood outside the thick plastic observation window, quiet for the first few moments. Inside the chamber, the technicians directed Schwab to lie on a long table. Once they had him in position, they moved the scanner head—a two-meter globe with a flat bottom—over the table, checking its alignment with Schwab and the table.

Next to him, Benson heard McMasters shifting his feet impatiently. "Why do you always insist on watching this part, Benson? Those technicians never make mistakes."

"They made a mistake in *People vs. Samuelson*."

"Once, they made a mistake."

"For Samuelson, once was enough. He's walking the streets. All it takes is one mistake, the right mistake."

"And just because of Samuelson, they don't make those mistakes any more. Because of him, they're more critical of the entire process. They try to catch errors before they happen."

"They may not succeed. No one's perfect."

McMasters grunted, an ambiguous, noncommittal grunt, as though he thought very little of Benson's theory of human imperfection but had no ready facts to combat it.

Both men returned to watching the technicians.

The technicians finished setting up the equipment. One of them turned toward an associate in the scan control room and gave a thumbs-up gesture, then repeated the gesture to Benson and McMasters. McMasters started down the corridor without a word.

Benson followed, still thinking about Schwab's story. If Schwab was telling the truth, all Benson's attention to detail might turn out to be meaningless. No matter how he succeeded in getting the tape cut and edited, there would still be enough on it to convict the man. If all the evidence pointed reasonably to Schwab's guilt, where did that leave Benson's emotional reaction to his client? His commitment to him?

Benson put the question out of his mind. Some things were better looked at after the fact than anticipated ahead of time. He followed McMasters into the discovery room, a small, white-walled room with a set of matched consoles for prosecution and defense. The holographic playback cubes at eye level on the consoles remained opaque. Benson took up his place at the defense console, easing his bulk into the contour chair and relaxing for the first time that day.

McMasters, sitting alertly at the prosecution console, glanced at Benson. "You're looking a little ill, Brother Benson. Anything serious?"

"Just a cold. It keeps hanging on."

"You're sure it's nothing serious?"

"I'm sure."

Editing a kineticorder tape was always the hardest part of a trial for Benson. He had to keep in mind his client's explanation of what happened, the legal overtones of the entire situation, what the other side would try to make out of it and what the prosecution's probable point of attack would be. At the same time, he had to relate, with some sensitivity, the events on the holographic display cube to his other considerations. Most of all, he had to gain an overall impression of the tape and the effect that impression would create on a jury. The process demanded total concentration.

McMasters had the same consideration. Presumably, he thought that rattling Benson before the editing began, no matter how slightly, might provide some sort of advantage. Benson had expected a ploy along those lines, but only somewhat later in the session, not at the beginning.

McMasters scrutinized Benson, examining his face with what he evidently thought was a clinical eye. "It looks like something a little more serious than a cold, Brother Benson. Are you sure you don't want to postpone the reading until you're in better shape?"

Benson looked up from the green objection plate he had been idly examining in a futile effort to avoid conversation with McMasters. "I'm fine, McMasters, just fine. I'll worry about my health and you worry about your case."

"I can't think of a better way to work things. You take care of your business and I'll take care of mine. But, of course, we still have this fellow Schwab to worry about together, don't we? I mean, we will have to be on speaking terms."

"Did someone say we weren't on speaking terms?"

"Your tone of voice—"

"It's probably the cold. I want to make this go as smoothly as possible. If we can both sheathe our rapierlike wits for a while, I think we can do that."

Immediately, Benson felt dissatisfied with himself. He should have ignored McMasters. McMasters would have run down by himself if Benson had let the conversation die at the beginning. It seldom paid to let needling get under the skin. That McMasters had succeeded, however slightly, indicated the cold was indeed having some effect on Benson's judgment.

He had thought, after a bit, that McMasters had given up needling. The prosecutor's next remark, however, delivered in a condescending tone, indicated he had only changed his point of attack, substituting the state of Benson's legal knowledge for the state of his health. "You're right, Brother Benson, personal remarks are out of place here. Let's talk about this criminal telepath of yours. The man interests me, as does the crime. I'm sure you know the history of the legislation as well as I do but. . . ."

McMasters began a short recital of the legislation behind the criminal telepathy statute. Granting that Benson knew as much about it as McMasters, the prosecutor intended to go right ahead and explain it, in case—or so said the inference in McMasters's tone—Benson had failed to do his homework. Benson allowed McMasters to plod through his opening comments—the federation population increase that also increased the once-in-a-half-billion telepathic births, the growing need to outlaw the willful application of psionic force to another mind, a comment about the common law's genius for adaptability, "new crimes for new times, Brother Benson."

Fortunately, before Benson had to endure too much of the prosecutor's lecture, the yellow ready lights came on in front of them. McMasters noticed them and shook his head, annoyed at the interruption but turning his attention to the console and the clearing holocube before him. The beginning of the kineticorder scan could not have been better timed.

Benson sat back in his chair, hiding his relief. Talking to McMasters, even when they met socially, was always difficult. The man's pretensions, annoying enough in casual conversation, took on a magnified quality when they were presented in an adversary setting, particularly when Mc-Masters was trying to show his scholarly erudition.

Benson directed his attention at the cube, trying to exclude irrelevant thoughts about McMasters. Vague shapes moved and twisted within the cube, the computer zeroing in on those few hours Schwab spent on Paria. Benson concentrated on the forming images.

"Aha!" said McMasters as the shapes resolved.

Benson ignored the attempted distraction and settled

down to watch the reading, his hand over the glowing objection plate. He would try to fill in the gaps in what he saw with what Schwab had told him.

It was raining on Paria. Schwab sat in a chair in his hotel room, legs crossed, his weight shifted onto one hip, his chin cupped in his hand. The rain outside made dirty tracks on the plastic window. A street outside, barely more than a rutted dirt road, showed irregular puddles and mud. Across the street, a warehouse looked dull and drab. Even a row of elms, evidently someone's addition to a homey Earth atmosphere, looked faded and drooping. Benson tried to adjust the color contrast on the cube.

The console responded by superimposing "Adjustment Correct" on the action in the cube.

McMasters noticed Benson's hand on the adjustment plate. "It's the sunlight, Brother Benson. That's an F spectra star. Everything looks dull in that light."

The remark caught Benson off guard. In spite of the man's pretensions, Benson had to admit the prosecutor had done his homework. But was there anything more to the remark? Had McMasters let it slip as a test? Showing some of his expertise on the planet's background might be McMasters's way of testing Benson's own preparation. Benson decided to remain impassive, letting McMasters believe whatever he chose. He returned his attention to the cube.

The rain stopped. The dingy sun steamed the flatlands outside the hotel window. In the distance, Benson could make out the native mounds, humps in the landscape. He could see a few of the creatures beginning to emerge from their mounds to rebuild after the rain. The gray creatures, able to form natural scoops with their forehands, had covered half of Paria's warm belt with underground networks and the occasional eruptions of mounds. The Parians probably wondered what the Earthmen wanted with the dirt they considered only a by-product of their tunneling.

Even the gross exploitation of the situation—the exchange of ore for tools designed on Earth for Parian use, tools to dig pyraclore ore more efficiently—would be meaningless to them. They would dig whether or not Earthmen wanted the by-product. They no doubt felt—if they thought about such things—that the Earthmen were the ones being exploited.

In the cube's replay of events Schwab stood and paced the hotel room. He looked around, as if expecting to find someone else in the room.

"Objection!" shouted McMasters, simultaneously slamming his hand down on the objection plate in front of him. The cube went blank. A small yellow light on Benson's console lit up, echoing McMasters by reading "objection."

Benson glanced at McMasters, annoyed. "To what, for heaven's sake? All he's done is stand up. I can't see anything objectionable—legally or otherwise—in that."

"I object to this whole business," answered McMasters, "of your man standing around doing nothing. It's immaterial, irrelevant and entirely beside the point. It goes."

"It stays."

"Why? It doesn't show anything. Your man's just standing there doing absolutely nothing except—"

"Minding his own business."

McMasters grunted, evidently contemptuous of the idea of minding one's own business. "Hardly relevant."

"Will you take a computer ruling on it or do we have to find a judge?"

McMasters thought, probably trying to ferret out any possible ulterior motive on Benson's part. Finally, he nodded, willing to let the computer rule on the material. "I'll rely on the computer's judgment. I have no doubt which way it will go."

Benson touched a plate marked "objection evaluation." The computer's voice, a neutral voice neither identifiably male nor female, responded: "The material is judged to be irrelevant and immaterial and will be stricken from tape seventy-two forty-six, Schwab, Ernest J."

McMasters smiled, self-satisfaction evident on his face. He clearly enjoyed his minuscule victory. He raised his chin slightly. "Shall we proceed, Brother Benson?"

Annoyed, Benson nodded. That the computer sustained the objection meant nothing one way or another. If necessary, the computer's ruling could always be appealed to a human judge and beyond to higher courts. Still, it annoyed Benson. The moment he heard the ruling, he knew McMasters had set up the situation as another test, or to gain some small psychological advantage.

Yet there was some significance in McMasters's timing. He had objected only when Schwab stood up and looked around. At that moment, Schwab said he had begun to feel as though someone were watching him. Schwab described it as the feeling one has in crowds occasionally when you can sense someone watching you but are unable to pinpoint who. In this case, Schwab was utterly alone. McMasters's objection, timed to coincide with the inception of Schwab's malaise, could have more to it than its superficial significance. Was the objection solely a test of Benson, or did it have some reference to the case itself?

Benson decided to try and speed up the process. He glanced at McMasters. "Look, McMasters, we're going to be here all day if you keep objecting to every blink of an eye. I'm prepared to stay here all day, if that's what it takes—"

"I'm glad to hear that, Brother Benson."

"But why don't we just get one run straight through—without objections—and see what we have. We can cut and splice later."

McMasters shook his head, a look of mock perplexity on his face, as if wondering at this unlawyerlike attitude in his colleague. "All right, Brother Benson. If you just want to sit here like we're out for an afternoon's entertainment, that's perfectly all right with me, but a timely objection now will save us time later. We won't have to go over the whole damn thing a dozen times. But since I have a fairly good idea what the tape is going to show—"

"What?"

"Your man in the process of mindwiping Jeremy Morris. I have no objection to letting any of it in."

McMasters turned back to his console, pushing the objection release plate. The computer noted his consent to continue the reading. The cube came to life.

Schwab paced the hotel room, occasionally glancing at the streaked window. Benson watched as the events unfolded, presented substantially as Schwab had told them in the cell. At one point, when Schwab left his hotel room and started down the corridor, McMasters muttered, "Ah, now we're getting somewhere." On the tape, Schwab entered Governor Morris's office, stood a moment behind the governor and—

The cube went blank, this time without the objection light coming on. Benson glanced at McMasters, noticing the prosecutor's finger on the hold plate.

"That, Brother Benson, is Jeremy Morris. And in his case, youth was a decided advantage. Do you know anything about that man's background? Do you know anything about what was wiped out of existence with him?"

Benson knew Governor Morris's background as well as did McMasters. In spite of that, he let the prosecutor continue. It would be quicker to let McMasters give his "poor victim" speech—a speech he probably delivered twice a week—than to argue about getting back to the tape and then have to listen to the speech anyway. "I'm sure you're going to tell me all about it."

McMasters, either missing or ignoring the sarcasm in Benson's voice, began as though reciting from memory, probably repeating the details from some investigator's report. "Jeremy Morris, New Harvard class of '09, New

Harvard Law class of '12, representative from the planet of Pylos Four to the federation on Earth at the age of 28 and Governor of the Parian Concession under special directive from Federation President Stacy at age 30. In short, Brother Benson, a brilliant and accomplished man, whom this . . . this . . . *telepath*—" McMasters spat out the word "—whom you're representing mindwiped down to a fetus. The people on your side of the court never consider things like that, do they, Brother Benson? They never consider the victim. It's always the rights of the accused and nothing else. For the love of Zeus, how I wish you people would open your eyes. If you ever saw—really saw—what your clients do to society—to people—you might get off your almighty self-righteous hobbyhorses about the rights of the accused and start paying attention to reality. We might start putting away a few of these psychopaths—and telepaths—instead of loosing them on society to commit their crimes again and again."

"I'm not aware of any empirical studies that show criminal telepaths have a high recidivism."

"Not aware! Something like 60 percent of the crimes committed within federation jurisdiction are recidivist crimes, committed by people released back into society by the efforts of you and your brethren defense counsel. If that isn't empirical enough for you—"

"I was talking about criminal telepaths, not burglars."

"Criminals are criminal, even telepathic ones."

"Are you finished?"

"No."

"Then please hurry up and do so. My stomach says we're getting close to lunch."

"I hope they give this man Schwab the whole Rehab treatment. I hope they wipe him as clean as he wiped that fine young Morris. I hope they rebuild his personality with a homophobic syndrome so strong he'll tremble with fear every time he comes within two meters of another human.

I hope the only thing that's left of him when they finish is—"

"*I* hope you finish this election speech before lunch."

McMasters grunted, at last sensing Benson's lack of interest. "Am I boring you?"

"Someone once asked Aristotle the same question. He answered 'No, I wasn't listening.' "

McMasters grunted again.

Benson glanced at McMasters's finger on the hold plate.

McMasters, following the direction of Benson's glance, glanced at his own finger a moment, then at Benson as though deciding whether to continue his harangue or remain silent. He lifted his finger from the plate.

The cube filled with the interior of Governor Morris's office on Paria. Schwab, still standing behind the governor, bent forward slightly.

"That," said McMasters, almost gloating, "was when your telepath did it."

At last Schwab stood erect. He seemed to waver a moment as if about to collapse. At that moment, the name—Regina—had come into his mind. Schwab staggered toward the door, hesitated a moment, looked around as if in search of something and paused to rub his temples.

Benson was about to push the hold plate, hoping to cut the reading short before Curly Curtis, the man Schwab called from the office, became implicated. Just then, McMasters broke in. "I don't think we need much more—" he glanced at Benson, a look of assurance on his face "—for a conviction. You may concede at any time, Brother Benson. Someone will contact me in the event you actually want to do such a thing." McMasters scrutinized Benson's face. When he spoke, he momentarily dropped the lawyer façade. "But I don't suppose you'll actually want to do that, will you? You'll carry the whole thing through to the bitter end. I doubt it will help your reputation, Brother Benson."

Benson reached over and tapped the hold plate, sitting back in his chair and watching McMasters. "What did you have in mind?"

"I wasn't talking about a plea bargain, Benson. I was talking about your attitude. I don't intend to make any deals on this one." McMasters gestured toward the holocube. "I can already see by this tape that I've got a conviction. I can't see any reason to deal anything out with evidence like that. One look and the jury will jump my way."

"You have evidence my man was in the room. That's it. I can't see that tape establishing a cause and effect relationship between Schwab and the mindwiping any more than his presence on the planet. Maybe Schwab just happened to be in the office when it occurred."

McMasters gave a sneering smile. "And maybe I'm just hanging around this prison facility for laughs."

"The man says he's innocent."

"They all say they're innocent."

"I believe him."

"I don't. There's only one deal I'll make in this case, Benson. You plead your telepath guilty as charged and I'll recommend immediate rehabilitation, the sooner the better."

Benson smiled weakly. "Not much of a deal."

"It's the only deal he deserves." McMasters's face became intense. He leaned toward Benson. "And all he deserves—no more, no less. I've spent too many years dealing out people a rap on the knuckles instead of a kick in the teeth. Either he pleads guilty as charged or we take it all the way to the jury. Why in hell's name are you asking for anything else?"

"That's what I get paid for, keeping you honest. They pay me to take it all the way to the end, if that's what's necessary."

McMasters shook his head, unable to comprehend why

anyone would work the defense side of the criminal docket. Still shaking his head in mock bewilderment, he stood up. "If you change your mind—or if talking to him—" McMasters indicated the blank holocube "—changes your mind, my office will put you through to me."

"You're not going to watch the arrest?"

"No. I've seen the arresting officer's tape. He acted correctly. I'll have my version of the tape sent over to your office. After I look at your version, I'm sure we'll have a little chat. Until then, good afternoon, Brother Benson."

McMasters walked through the doorway of the discovery room, his bearing confident.

Benson looked back at the cube. He touched the hold release plate. The holocube cleared. The scan continued through Schwab's call to Curly Curtis, his departure from the hotel, his trip to the ore shuttle with Curtis and his return to the hotel. This last detail confirmed Benson's judgment of Schwab, who would never have returned to the hotel if he felt himself responsible for the mindwiping. He would have stayed on the shuttle and escaped. When Schwab left the hotel a second time and started out toward the Parian mounds, Benson touched the call plate that connected the discovery room with the technicians in the scanning chamber. "This is Benson. Please take a reading through the arrest and have the tape sent to my office. Thank you."

He would go over the last few minutes of the tape that night, examine it with minute care. His cold, already giving him a headache, would interfere. Still, the effort had to be made. He might find an apparently insignificant but crucial detail. If so, Benson wished the detail would present itself as soon as possible. He could see very little ahead for Schwab but conviction.

CHAPTER 6

Benson sat alone in his office. His partners and secretary had gone home. Before his secretary left, she had stacked a neat pile of record cards on his desk. He would have to spend half the night going through them, longer to evaluate them.

Resigning himself to the drudgery, he slid back the top of his desk and activated the document reader. He took a deep breath and tried to clear his throat. The cold was worse. It felt as if someone had worked over the inside of his throat with a scrub brush.

He inserted the first slick card in the slot next to the screen, then reached for the phone on top of the desk. He punched in the local number of the federation records computer, along with his federation bar number and the firm's account number for later billing.

A light came on at the top of the screen, indicating a clear line to the computer.

"Records," said Benson, his voice scratchy, "collate the following data with all relevant federation records, civil and criminal. I am prepared to wait for a level five search."

"Yes, sir," responded the computer.

A second light lit by the screen, indicating the search had begun. Benson sat back and watched the screen. The first of the documents appeared. Benson examined it briefly and pushed the negative plate. The next document appeared. After the first ten minutes, tired, bored and his nose feeling more stuffed up because of the inactivity, Benson had to force himself to pay attention. Court orders, appellate decisions, administrative orders, even pleadings and arguments of counsel, flashed on the screen. A level five search included everything related to the topic not strictly classified as secret. Each time a new document came on the screen, Benson glanced over it and touched the negative plate, discarding it. Each time, another appeared, equally irrelevant to Benson's purposes.

Though he was examining only a minute portion of the vast federation records system—so small a part as to be almost statistically meaningless—it seemed to Benson as the minutes and hours passed as though he had been condemned by a pitiless god to a bureaucratic hell, forced to examine every record ever kept in the history of mankind. Each time it came to nothing.

Finally, past midnight, a document caught his attention. He pushed the hold plate and examined it more closely. Satisfied, he touched the printout plate and waited for his copy of the document—a 24-year-old court order—to slide from the slot at the base of the phone.

He reread it and touched the command plate for direct access to the computer. "Records, give me a printout on any information relating to one Regina Quinton." He spelled the name. "She was a resident of the city of New Los Angeles on Wolff-74-5, about 20 years ago."

Two minutes elapsed. The computer responded by printing out half a dozen documents on a single sheet of phone-fax paper. Benson watched the long tongue of paper extrude from below the phone, spilling into a basket.

The paper stopped.

"All data under that name. Would you desire information under another name or combination of names?"

"No, thank you."

For the next half hour, Benson read the documents, then rose and paced his office. He glanced at his watch— 00:30. McMasters might still be awake. He returned to his desk and punched out McMasters's home number. It rang several times.

At last, McMasters answered, his face deeply lined on the screen. Benson wondered momentarily whether Mc-Masters used some kind of cosmetic during the day, an effort to keep his look of distinguished middle age unsullied by the fact of advancing old age.

McMasters frowned. "Benson, it's—" he glanced off camera at a clock "—almost one in the morning. Can't whatever it is wait?"

"I'm afraid not." Benson tried to make his voice sound as hoarse as possible. It took little effort. He also let his face go slack, adding to the ill appearance. The effect, he noticed, showed in the monitor screen. "I think you were right about my health, McMasters. This cold's doing me in. I'd like to take you up on that postponement. I've been getting worse all day."

McMasters became suspicious, eyes narrowing. "What is this, Benson? Some kind of trick? This afternoon you told me to mind my own business when I asked about your health. Now, you want a postponement based on it. Absolutely not. Due process demands we get this over with as quickly as possible."

In spite of McMasters's dogmatic answer, Benson knew the prosecutor was only sounding him out, trying to determine what, if anything, was in back of Benson's request. There was no legal way Benson could get a postponement short of physical illness. McMasters would either have to buy the cold excuse or Benson would have to think up something more drastic.

"In all fairness," began Benson, trying to instil as much of a nasal quality as possible into his voice, "you must realize this is a complicated matter. If I have to hand it over to someone else in the office while I recuperate, it might take twice as long for them to become acquainted with the details. Just agreeing to a postponement would simplify matters, and save time in the long run. I want to get this over with as quickly as you do, but I also want my man to have the fairest possible chance. I'm sure you'd agree with that. I can't give him my best efforts if I'm plugged up from ear to ear."

"Is this some kind of tactical maneuver to benefit that mindwiper of yours?"

"What possible advantage could I gain by it?"

"Time. Time's always an advantage."

"Two weeks? How much of an advantage is that? A week for my cold and a week to catch up on my other work."

McMasters thought about the proposition. Benson could almost read the man's thoughts, those of any lawyer in the same situation, gauging possibilities. "All right, Benson, but on one condition."

"What's that?"

"You won't try for bail."

"I wouldn't get it even if I tried."

"I'm glad we agree on that. This telepath stays in jail and you have two weeks."

McMasters hung up.

Benson immediately punched out the number of the federation detention facility. The night sergeant's ruddy face appeared on the screen. "Security sector four, Sergeant Webly speaking."

"Put me through to Schwab, Ernest J., seven two, four six."

The screen went blank. A few moments later the trace light on Benson's phone glowed briefly, indicating Sergeant Webly had not only checked Benson's name and voiceprint against those on file for Schwab's attorney, but had traced back the number as well. It irritated Benson to have his word doubted, but Webly was only doing his job.

At last, Schwab's face came on the screen.

Benson started talking immediately. "I'm afraid you're going to be in jail a little longer than we hoped. I just arranged for a postponement. It will put the trial off at least another two weeks. Can you handle that?"

"Two weeks! Of this!"

"It's a short enough time, Schwab."

"On the outside, it's short. In here, it's forever."

Benson could see depression begin to set in on Schwab's face when the latter shook his head. "I don't suppose it matters much, Mr. Benson. As long as I'm here, I'm not in a rehab center."

"Forget about that for now, Schwab. I've been checking the public record. I've come up with something that may help us. It's not much, but it's the only thing I can see right now that we've got to work with."

"And?"

"I think I've found Regina."

Schwab's eyes brightened. "You found her. Where? Who is she? Where is she?"

"I found evidence of her, that's all."

"What evidence?"

"Regina Quinton. She was once sued by the city of New Los Angeles on Wolff-74-5. It was a little over 20 years ago. She was a five-year-old girl. But it forced her parents to move her outside the city. The injunction read something to the effect that as long as such condition shall continue, said Regina Quinton shall not be allowed to be present within the City of New Los Angeles for a period exceeding three hours daily."

"What condition? Was she a leper?"

"Worse, an emitter-telepath."

"What's an—" Schwab looked momentarily uncomfortable "—emitter-telepath?"

"The tests they took on you," continued Benson, "show you as *receptively* sensitive. Most telepaths are receptives.

One in 100 emits thoughts that normal. . . ." Benson hesitated, regretting the word. "I mean, non-telepathic people hear, if hear's the right word. As children, they can't control it any more than children can control most things about themselves. They're like psy-foghorns in the head of anyone within a kilometer. You can imagine what a five-year-old thinks about. If you lived in the area of the five-year-old emitter-telepath—especially *you*—you'd think about it, too—whether you wanted to or not. So they got an injunction against her coming into the city. Otherwise, she probably would have paralyzed the entire city and had them all mumbling about dolls or tricycles or whatever five-year-olds think about."

Schwab, following Benson with close attention, smiled slightly. "I imagine that interfered with business."

"Everything but the tricycle business."

"So you're going to Wolff-74-5."

"No. Paria."

THE next morning, Benson made arrangements for the trip to Paria. He turned over any matters that needed immediate attention to his partners. They grumbled at the increased workload, but accepted it, knowing Benson would do the same if their situations were reversed. His secretary made reservations on the afternoon shuttle, then on the interstellar liner *Liberty*. Once in the general area of Paria, Benson would have to transfer from the liner to a Diversicorp freighter. Passenger starships seldom visited Paria.

Confirming the travel arrangements took most of the morning. Finally, he was able to leave the office and go home to pack. He had filled two suitcases when the phone glowed. He left the suitcases on the bed and crossed the room to answer it.

A man's face, vigorous and middle-aged, appeared on the screen. "Mr. Benson, my name is Cowdin. I understand from your office that you are planning a trip to Paria."

Benson made a noncommittal response, wanting to find out more about the man before he said anything.

"It is my home planet, Mr. Benson. Actually, my adopted home planet. I was born here on Earth. I would like to offer you any assistance I can to make your journey more fruitful."

"Such as?"

Cowdin shrugged. "Anything. Information about Paria, or the people there, both the government and Diversicorp people. That sort of thing. Paria is a small place. Anyone who lives there can tell you anything you might want to know about anyone else."

Something about the man's presence on the screen—combined with the unexpected call—made Benson uneasy. "How did you happen to contact me, Mr. Cowdin?"

"You *do* represent Ernest Schwab?"

"Yes."

"I thought so. Tragic what's happened, isn't it? I was here on Earth—I run most of the mining operations on Paria for Diversicorp, by the way—I was here conducting some business and read about Schwab's difficulty."

"Do you know Mr. Schwab?"

"Not personally, but he does work for the same company I do. I would like to offer you any help I can on Schwab's behalf."

"I would think—since Paria is such a small place—that you would be doing everything you could to make sure Mr. Schwab is convicted. I understand Governor Morris was well liked by the people there."

Cowdin smiled. "Not by everyone, Mr. Benson. I, of course, had nothing personal against Governor Morris, but he did have enemies on Paria."

Benson started to speak.

Cowdin interrupted. "Oh, it's no great secret, Mr. Benson. Morris and I did not get along. Frankly, it was both official and personal. I believe—though I have very little evidence to back it up—that Governor Morris was trying to close down my company's operations on Paria. That would have been unfortunate. He hampered me at every turn, always coming up with new rules, new regulations, new forms and permits. There are only a few thousand people on the entire planet. If Morris had continued with his red tape campaign, ninety percent of them would have been involved in a paper shuffling bureaucracy."

"Then you're glad he's out of the way."

"Of course. I would not have done anything about removing him—at least nothing along the line of this mindwiping—but I can't honestly say I'm sorry it happened. I believe Morris threw up that wall of paper just to keep my company from carrying out its lawful operations—and all of those operations, Mr. Benson, were approved by the Federation Interstellar Development Bureau. I believe Morris was trying to go against their judgment. Since he could not do it directly, he did it by harassing us."

"You said some of your dislike of Morris was personal."

Cowdin smiled. "I'm sure you've been filled in on Morris. The brilliant young man, the man with a future, the pride of the federation and—to hear some people talk—a possible future president of the federation. I'm also sure there are people who believe it, even people who actually knew Morris. But—" Cowdin waved his hand, brushing aside the question "—no, let's let bygones be bygones, Mr. Benson. Why defame the—why defame people who cannot defend themselves? In any case, let me offer you my services. I think Mr. Schwab should be given the fairest possible opportunity to present his side of the case in court. Frankly, I can understand why someone with Mr. Schwab's talent—if that's what you call the result of one wild gene—would use his ability against

Morris. That doesn't mean I condone it, but I do understand."

"Schwab doesn't."

"Oh?"

Cowdin let the question hang in midair, probably hoping to gain more information. Benson ignored it. "I do have a shuttle to catch, Mr. Cowdin."

Cowdin smiled again. "Yes, I understand. I'll be returning to Paria myself. If I can offer you any assistance, I'll be happy to do so."

"Thank you. I'll keep that in mind."

They hung up.

Benson stood a moment next to the phone, hand lingering near the buttons. Cowdin's call puzzled him. The man's profession of concern for Schwab's fair treatment, though admirable as an abstract principle, seemed somehow feigned. What other purpose could he have possibly had for the call? Benson could think of only one. For whatever reason, Cowdin may have wanted to have a look at Benson before they encountered each other on Paria.

BENSON took the monorail to the shuttleport. During the ride, he continued to puzzle over the call from Cowdin. The more he thought about it, the more pointless it seemed. Yet, a feeling persisted that the call was purposeful. Finally, he gave up worrying about it. Whatever the call meant, he would find out eventually.

The computer-guided car slid into a station two levels under the shuttleport. Soundlessly, the doors opened, letting in a rush of noise from the terminal, chattering voices punctuated by an occasional announcement over the public-address system. Benson carried his luggage across the platform, up the escalator, and along a moving belt through brightly lit corridors. When he arrived at the shuttle area designated on his ticket, he left his suitcases at the baggage check and wandered over to the nearest concession. Along with a disposable viewer, he brought three magazine tapes back to the shuttle boarding area, preparing to go through them during the hours between the shuttle's lift-off and the suspended animation couch on the *Liberty*.

He had inserted the first disk in the viewer and indexed it to the table of contents when he happened to look up. A figure had broken away from the group of approaching passengers and was approaching him. It took him several seconds to recognize Cowdin.

The mining engineer sat in a chair next to Benson and nodded. "Good to see you again. I think we're on the same run. The *Liberty*, isn't it?"

Benson nodded. "You completed your business sooner than you expected."

"On the contrary, Mr. Benson, I have had this return trip to Paria scheduled for some time. Connections to Paria are infrequent. I have to schedule my affairs around available transportation, not the other way around. It is—" he shrugged "—unfortunate, but Paria is a little-visited colony."

They sat in silence for several minutes. Eventually, Cowdin began to look uncomfortable, shifting from one side of his seat to the other. At last, he stirred and made a move to stand. "If you'll excuse me, Mr. Benson, I think I'll follow your example and buy some magazine disks while they are still available."

Cowdin strolled off in the direction of the magazine counter, his gait self-conscious, as though aware that Benson was watching.

Benson pocketed his magazine viewer and tapes, then stood and walked to the shuttle check-in counter. The shuttle service manager, a tall blonde with a name plate labeled "Louise," smiled at him and awaited his inquiry.

Benson nodded toward Cowdin, whose back was toward them. "My friend, Mr. Cowdin, over there is leaving on the shuttle that connects with the *Liberty*. He will have to transfer to a freighter at some point during the journey. He's worried about connections. He wanted me to check and see if they're in order."

"What is his ultimate destination?"

"A planet called Paria. I doubt if you've heard of—"

The woman smiled, nodding. "Oh, yes, I've heard of it. My husband once went there. He hated it. I don't think he ever got over the experience." She touched several buttons on a computer console, then spoke Cowdin's name and destination into the computer. It answered immediately, confirming Cowdin's reservations, then announced a series of numbers, significant to the woman but meaningless to Benson.

She nodded. "Your friend was lucky. He's booked through to Paria. He filled the last seat."

Benson smiled pleasantly, thanked her and returned to his chair in the waiting area. Cowdin, though claiming to have made his reservations well in advance, had actually made them after Benson. What that fact meant—if it meant anything more than a late decision on Cowdin's part to return to Paria—Benson found more difficult to say. Still, the possible connection with his own activities seemed too strong to ignore. But why would Cowdin follow—or, at least, accompany—him back to Paria? No answer came readily to mind.

Benson took out the viewer again. Just as he settled down to watch the magazine, the public address system announced the departure of his shuttle. He repocketed the viewer and pulled out his boarding pass, standing and walking to the shuttle boarding line. Ahead of him, he could see Cowdin just passing into the tunnel that led to the shuttle. Whatever the man had in mind, the trip promised to be interesting.

REGINA

I have seen no one since he left. Weeks must have passed since I last saw him. I lose track of time here. Weeks and days are the same. The computer has not come alive since he left. I cannot make it come alive. Only he knows how to do it. I can see the chintz frills around the edges of the computer. I should close the curtains. The pink, red and yellow pattern looks better than the bare machinery. The machines are not appropriate to my living quarters. They remind me of men and what men do. Men have never been kind to me. They have always set me apart from them. I am not bitter. I understand. It is their nature. But he and I will make them change.

CHAPTER 7

Schwab paced his cell. Benson's phone call had unsettled him. The prospect of spending two additional weeks
in the prison facility annoyed him. Worse than that, the
two weeks could prove useless. Benson might find nothing
of value on Paria. Schwab wanted to go with him. He
wanted to be able to help. After all, *he* had been on the
spot, not Benson.

Schwab smiled, a grim and ironic smile. On the spot.
It expressed how he felt. The feeling had grown steadily
from the moment of his arrest to the present. Even the
kineticorder session—designed, according to Benson, to
bring out the truth—had only made Schwab feel more on
the spot. When the loudspeaker in the kineticorder scanning chamber indicated the scan had been completed,
Schwab felt momentary relief. If anything Benson had said
proved accurate, the kineticorder might have picked up
something to help free him.

He had reached up and touched the buckle on his chest.
The straps had fallen away, clattering down the sides of
the table. He sat up and released the buckle on the straps
across his legs.

At first, he had been unable to distinguish the changed
quality of the voice from the speaker. "All right, Schwab,
get off the table and walk to the door. The two guards there
will accompany you back to your cell. Remember, they
are both armed with stunclubs. We want no incidents here.
They are authorized to totally paralyze you if necessary
for facility security. They have both set their stunclubs on

75

a deadman's grip. If either of them is rendered unconscious, the stunclubs will be activated and paralyze anyone
within 20 meters. Nod if you understand."

Frowning slightly, wondering about the extreme caution
shown in his handling, Schwab had nodded understanding.
He followed orders and walked to the door. The two
guards, each keeping a good distance between themselves
and Schwab, had accompanied him back to his cell. Once,
he had tried to make conversation, hoping to draw the men
out. The larger of the two had simply grunted and told
Schwab to keep walking.

While strapping Schwab onto the kineticorder scanning
table, the technicians had been talkative. Also, the single
guard who brought Schwab to the waiting area had been
equally talkative. But after the scan, an additional guard
was assigned to him and everyone had become cautious
and withdrawn. Just one explanation fit. Something on the
tape had changed their opinion. Instead of considering him
an ordinary prisoner in the facility, they now treated him
like a special exception. The technicians had monitored
the tape during the scan and something they saw alarmed
them. Before the scan, they had strapped him in. After
it, they were leery of even being in the same room with
him. As far as Schwab could tell, the tape would show
little more than his short walk down the hotel corridor
on Paria, a brief pause in Governor Morris's office and,
ultimately, his confused attempt to flee. How any of it
could cause this change in attitude was beyond him. If
the tape had shown an ax murder or a sadistic slow broil-
ing with a burnrifle, he would have been able to understand
their reaction.

In addition, the guards who accompanied him back to
his cell had exercised extreme caution. They had held their
stunclubs, each adjusted to the deadman setting, in prom-
inent view. Leading him back by a different route than

they had taken to the scanning chamber—presumably a more secure path than the original one—they had treated him like a vial of nitroglycerin. Each time he hesitated, they gruffly ordered him to move on. Once, he stopped intentionally to see whether they would shove him. They hung back, prodding him forward with words and the threat of the stunclub.

At last, arriving in front of his cell door, Schwab stopped and faced them. "What in the hell is the matter with you people? You act like I'm Typhoid Mary. I'm the same person you took out of this cell two hours ago, but you guys don't act like it."

The large guard, holding an electronic master key in his free hand, thumbed an index number on the key's touch plates. The cell door behind Schwab slid open. The guard nodded toward the open door. "Inside, mindwiper."

In that phrase, Schwab saw the reason for the guard's caution. If the tape had actually shown an ax murder, they would have known how to deal with him as a prisoner. Ax murderers, like most people, responded to the threat of a stunclub. They would have confidently brought him back to his cell and thought nothing more about it.

But Schwab was different. They had seen nothing on the tape. They had simply seen him standing in a room with a man who was later shown to have been mindwiped. To them, Schwab's reactions, unlike those of the ax murderer, were unpredictable. He was an enigma. On top of that, criminal telepaths—mindwipers—again unlike ax murderers, were allowed to keep their "ax" in jail, a part of their makeup unchanged by custody. As the cell door closed behind him, Schwab realized the reason behind their caution. The guards were afraid of being mindwiped.

At another time, the realization might have given Schwab a sort of grim satisfaction. He considered himself one of the least dangerous men he knew. Even Curly

Curtis, whose drunken sprees had got him transferred from starship duty to ground duty on Paria, was more dangerous than Schwab.

If the guards and technicians reacted that way to Schwab, how would a jury react? The guards and technicians associated with criminals every day, often on a personal basis. Yet they reacted to Schwab as though he *were* a criminal. A jury would have a more intense reaction. In their fear of what they thought of as his special powers, they would pay little attention to the facts. They would want him convicted before they even got to the facts. He had only one hope—Benson.

Schwab paced the cell. What could Benson hope to find on Paria? When he called, he mentioned a Regina Quinton. Until the moment of the mindwiping, Schwab had never heard the name. Only Benson had provided a last name to go with it. The name seemed to have no relation to him at all. What if Benson turned up nothing? They would be in exactly the same position as before his trip.

The answers to his questions were clear. If Benson failed, Schwab would be sent to a rehabilitation center, either on Earth or elsewhere. They would do to him with technology what they claimed he had done to Morris. They would mindwipe him. Not because of any primitive sense of vengeance, an eye for an eye. Nor from any sense of irony, though Schwab recognized that some people might consider it ironic that a criminal telepath should be mindwiped. But as part of the standard procedure for dealing with severe antisocials.

The thought chilled him. After rehabilitation, there would be nothing left of the Ernest Schwab he had become over the years. Only an artificial set of values, goals and motives would remain, shaped to a new standard of conduct. But men, working to duplicate nature, were less thorough than nature. Nature wanted a creature that could survive. Men wanted only someone who would avoid making trouble. The few rehabs Schwab had met were incapable of anything but marking time until they died. They could hold routine jobs to earn a living but they were without anything like a will of their own. Self-assertion after rehabilitation was unknown. His life would be the same outside the prison as inside. Things would happen around him. He would cause nothing to happen. He would become a model citizen.

In spite of its high probability of coming true, Schwab mentally blocked out this prediction of his future. For the hundredth time, he let his thoughts go over the events on Paria, hoping to uncover something he might have missed before. He remembered the landing on Paria, the hotel, the mindwiping. He remembered hiding in the warehouse, going to the shuttle with Curly, returning to the hotel. It was all so familiar, so vivid. None of it contained anything new. He remembered the confusion on his return to the hotel, his attempt to escape, his futile run through the tunnels and his final exhausted submission to Officer Daniels and the Parians. Reliving it, he could almost feel the chill in the tunnels, smell the stench of the Parians, experience his despair when he saw the footprint in the dust that told him he had been running in circles. The footprint. . . .

Something about the footprint struck his mind. He concentrated on it, trying to recall the exact image it had left in his memory.

Schwab sat down on his bunk, dropping his face to his hands in an effort to concentrate. He tried to visualize the scene as completely as possible.

Abruptly, Schwab sat bolt upright on the bunk. He had been concentrating so hard on the single footprint that he had missed the others, those he had made when he arrived at the spot for what he thought was the second time. Not footprint, but footprints. His own boots, designed for maximum traction on the metal and plastic surfaces of a starship, left a pattern of dots in the area of the sole and heel. The footprint he had found in the tunnel had a knobby pattern, as though designed for walking on rocks and dirt.

Schwab stood up He had to tell Benson No—he had to go to Paria and help Benson. He could not stand by, helpless, unable to contribute to his own defense. He could not leave it to anyone else. One of the few things he had learned during his years as a starship hand was the value of doing things himself. In space, that sort of self-reliance often meant the difference between life and death. Twice in his career, he had found himself outside a ship in a malfunctioning spacesuit. Each time, a rescue party had been sent. In both cases, if he had waited for the rescue party—waited for others to act for him and save him—he would have died. His own resourcefulness—once plugging a defective heater unit with the cement he had been using on the ship's hull and once opening a cargo hold manually from the outside—had saved him.

No one had escaped from a federation prison facility for about 100 years. The prisons were thought to be escapeproof. No man could. . . .

"No *man* said Schwab aloud.

Schwab stood up and resumed his pacing. He had to think things through. The guards, at least since the kineticorder session had become common knowledge, had treated him as anything but a man—more like a dangerous weapon about to be turned against them. In their eyes, he was not a man at all, but a telepath, something unpredictable. They were afraid of him. They had him surrounded by the most secure prison facility ever invented by man—yet they were afraid.

Schwab walked to the door and hit the callplate next to it After several seconds, the guard's cautious face appeared on the small screen, frowning and gruff.

"What is it, Schwab?"

"I want to talk to the watch commander

"Why?"

"I'll tell him that."

"You'll tell me that or you won't talk to him.'

"Listen, my lawyer said I have the right to talk to the watch commander. If you don't let me talk to him, I'll hav to—"

"Okay, okay, hold your horses. I'll get him."

The screen went blank. During the short interval between he guard's disappearance and the watch commander's appearance, Schwab felt himself becoming nervous. Briefly, he wondered whether he had the courage to go through with what he planned. He remembered the almost superhuman effort it had taken to open the starship cargo hold from the outside. This had saved his life then; he would have to keep that in mind during the next few hours.

The watch commander's round face appeared on the screen, looking as though he had been roused from a d ep sleep. His voice was blustery and irritated.

"What is it, Schwab?"

Schwab launched into his demands withou preliminary. "I want a reaction copter waiting outsid the main office of this facility within ten minutes I want—"

The watch commander shoo off his lingering air of sleep. "You want what?"

"A reactior copter then—"

"Wait a second, Schwab. What a you talking—"

"I want all nonessential personnel to be cleared from this area and all personnel unnecessary to shuttle lift-off removed from the area of the shuttleport. If these things are not done immediately, I intend to mindwipe everyone in this facility, guards, prisoners and anyone else within a half-kilometer range. If there is any delay or interference, I will do it instantaneously. Do you understand?"

The watch commander's eyes had grown progressively

larger. When Schwab finished, the man swallowed once before speaking.

"I don't have the authority to—"

"Get it."

"But—"

"No buts. And remember, if I see anything—and I mean anything—out of line, *everyone*—" Schwab swept his arm around in an arc, indicating the half-kilometer circle "—gets it." Schwab hit the callplate, breaking the connection.

He took a deep breath and discovered he was sweating. Still, in spite of the tension—perhaps because of it—he felt excited, almost giddy. In the weeks since being taken into custody, he had taken his first positive act. Right or wrong, he was no longer sitting around waiting for others to rescue him. He was moving events, making decisions and directing the situation. It was a good feeling. It added confidence to his already suffering ego, and confidence was the one quality he would need to get him safely to Paria. He did not concern himself with the consequences of his actions. Innocent men did not—at least in any proper system of justice—belong in prison.

The callplate glowed.

Schwab walked back to the door and touched it on. The watch commander's face, pallid now, reappeared on the screen.

"All right, Schwab. We have arranged everything. Your cell door will unlock automatically in—" the watch commander glanced off camera, evidently at a clock "—two minutes. Walk down the corridor to the far end and through the door. After that, you know the way to the main offices."

"If there are any tricks—"

The man broke the connection.

Schwab waited out the two minutes, feeling butterflies in his stomach. He gathered up the few possessions he had in the cell, trying to distract himself. If he made it as far as the main office building, he would consider himself lucky. If he made it farther, he would be experiencing a miracle.

Exactly two minutes after the call, the cell door clicked and slid back. Schwab peered into the corridor, checking both directions. The other cells in the block were closed. He could see no sign of either guards or other prisoners. They had cleared the facility quickly.

Cautiously, he headed down the corridor toward the door, trying to imagine what the watch commander would do to counter the escape. Schwab could not imagine the man simply letting him walk t unopposed.

Schwab reached the door at the end of the corridor. It, too, proved to be open He stepped into the next stretch of corridor, flanked by cell doors and illuminated indirectly from above. At the halfway point with 20 meters still ahead of him, he began to hear the hissing, a slight noise almost drowned by his footsteps.

He stopped and looked up. Only a faint turbulence near the ceiling indicated the presence of the gas. Schwab gulped as much air as possible and began to sprint toward the door at the far end of the corridor. He hoped he could reach it before he inhaled too much of the gas. After several meters, his exertion forced him to breath. He could smell the gas, a faint, perfumed quality added to the normal smells of the corridor, as though a woman had recently walked down the hall. He felt his head begin to lighten. Spots appeared before his eyes, stars of light that refused to vanish when he blinked.

He covered his mouth with his forearm, trying to breathe through just the cloth of his uniform, and then only when he could no longer hold his breath. His legs were beginning to feel rubbery. He had to concentrate to keep his balance. He staggered and fell.

Straining against his fading consciousness, Schwab pushed up from the floor onto his knees. The sweet flavor of the gas increased with every reluctant breath. He rose to his feet, staggering from side to side, expending more energy to keep upright than to move forward. His goal, the door, had blurred in front of him. He blinked, wide-eyed, to clear his eyes. The effort seemed to have no effect. The door remained a wavering form in front of him. He staggered toward it, one arm covering his mouth and nose, the other held in front of him in case he fell.

Abruptly, the last of his strength fading, his extended hand touched something. Blearily, Schwab stared ahead of him. The door—he had reached it. His hand groped for the touchplate and found it. He lay his palm across it.

The door failed to open.

CHAPTER 8

Schwab pounded on the door with the flat of his hand, hoping the noise might alert anyone on the other side. If they knew he had gotten this far, they might be intimidated. He felt the jolt of each resounding thump in his arm.

Unexpectedly, the door slid back, opened from the other side. Schwab staggered through to find himself facing four guards. They backed away from him, their hands held up at shoulder level.

Coughing and inhaling the fresh air, Schwab closed the door to the gas-filled corridor. When his head cleared and he felt he could stand without leaning against the door, he took a deep breath and nodded at the guards. "All right, down on your stomachs."

The men hesitated.

Schwab, knowing he had the advantage—the men had evidently decided to open the door, against orders, to save themselves from being mindwiped—scowled at them, looking from man to man and giving each a level stare.

Almost immediately, they obeyed him, lying face down on the floor.

"Hands behind your heads!" barked Schwab, feeling slightly uncomfortable that four armed men would lie face down on the orders of one unarmed person.

The men obeyed, covering the backs of their heads with their hands.

Schwab stood a moment, looking at them. Each carried a stunclub. He felt tempted to take one of the clubs. It would help him overcome the feeling of being naked in the face of a lurking army of armed men. Even more than the psychological boost, it would give him some actual protection. A stunclub's effective range, ten meters, might come in handy.

Schwab stepped up to the nearest man and reached for his stunclub, then hesitated. If he took the weapon, the fact would certainly be reported to the watch commander. The watch commander, according to Schwab's observations an intelligent enough man, might well start asking himself questions. He might ask why someone with the reputed ability to simultaneously mindwipe everyone in the facility would take any other weapon with him. At that point, the man might put two and two together and guess that Schwab was bluffing. Though it gave Schwab cold comfort to realize it, he knew he was safer unarmed than armed.

Schwab gathered up the stunclubs and made a show of standing in front of the prostrate guards and disarming each weapon, twisting the shank then pulling each apart and removing the powerpins. He dropped each useless club in front to the man who owned it. "If I see *any* of you people before I reach the copter, you'll be as lifeless as these stunclubs."

Schwab moved on. He followed the corridors toward the main office complex, passing kineticorder rooms, banks of cells and the recreation room—all empty of personnel or prisoners. At last, he reached the door leading into the open area between the cell blocks and the offices, a wide security strip called the "firebreak" by the guards. He paused at the door to catch his breath.

On the other side of the door would be more guards with stunclubs, possibly sharpshooters with knockout darts. The type of standoff Schwab was attempting could succeed only if no one fired, either intentionally or accidentally. Still, once committed, he could not draw back. He felt a temptation to throw his weight against the door and burst into the open area, then sprint for the offices on the other side. He restrained himself, stifling the urge. The same principle applied to this situation as to the guards in the corridor. If he walked purposefully across the security strip he would look more like a man who felt himself to have the upper hand. If he ran, someone would shoot.

Schwab touched the plate next to the door. The door slid back. Sunlight, bright and momentarily blinding, spilled into the room. Schwab waited for his eyes to adjust and started forward, walking down the concrete steps to the path across the security strip. With the first brush of a gentle breeze he realized how long he had been cooped up. If his attempt failed, it would have almost been worth it just for this brief time outdoors.

He glanced around at the open, empty area. Even on the walls that boxed the area into a sort of courtyard, he could see no guards. Then, unexpectedly, he saw something move on one corner of the walls, a shape followed by a slight flash of reflected sunlight. Schwab's nerve broke. Without thinking, he broke into a run, picking up speed and heading for the main office building.

At the instant he ran, the shape of a man moved. Standing up on the wall, his silhouette backlighted by the afternoon sun, he held a dart rifle against his shoulder. Schwab tried to run in a zigzag path, doubting the maneuver would interfere with the man's aim but hoping to give himself some kind of advantage Through his labored breathing, Schwab heard the distant *pompf* of the dart rifle, repeated almost immediately by another from a different direction. A dart—its arrowlike whish through the air clearly audible—passed his head. Another glanced from his shoe. He sprinted faster, at last reaching the door to the administration office. His hand reached out for the touch-plate then hesitated, as he sensed somewhere in the back of his mind the danger of laying his hand on the plate.

A dart slammed home in the spot where his hand would

have been, its tranquilizer fluid squirting from the needle point on impact. The dart clattered to the steps.

Sensing that no one had a direct bead on the touchplate now, Schwab pressed it, carefully avoiding the tranquilizer fluid. The door opened. He stepped inside. Another dart slammed into the closing door behind him.

Schwab glanced around the empty office. On one desk, a cup of coffee still steamed, evidence of the staff's quick exit. He walked to the desk and drank some of the coffee, then touched the nearest phone.

The watch commander, evidently expecting the call, came immediately on the screen.

Momentarily, Schwab felt tongue-tied, then summoned as authoritative a tone as possible and spoke, staring directly into the camera to give the effect of looking into the watch commander's eyes. "All right, I expected something like this. As you saw, I was able to deflect each of those darts. I restrained myself from anything more drastic by an effort of will. I have already warned you what will happen if you interfere with me. From now on, I want you to keep something clear in your mind. Do you know anything at all about telepathic mindwiping and what it can do?"

"Listen, Schwab—"

"You listen! Answer my question."

"No."

"I'm going to give you a very clear explanation so we won't have any misunderstanding with unfortunate results. Subjectively, I can set it to cover as broad or as narrow a range as I choose. It's like squinting your eyes to narrow the field of vision. Except it's automatic. I want you to understand that point completely. It's like a cocked gun, ready to go off at a moment's notice. The next time I get one whiff of gas or see one guard with a dart gun, it goes off. Do you understand?"

"Yes, but—"

"I told you, no buts. You didn't believe me the first time. Believe me this time. I'm leaving this place. Now. Either you cooperate or all of you are going to be empty husks." Schwab narrowed his eyes, squinting into the camera. "You will be the first to go. Is the copter ready?"

The watch commander stared a moment, thinking, making up his mind. Schwab had no idea whether any telepath could function in the manner he had just described. Still, the reality of the situation mattered very little. The longer Schwab was involved with the authorities, the more he realized how little it had ever mattered. Only what people believe to be reality—the jury, the watch commander— mattered.

Finally, the resignation visible in his face, the watch commander nodded. "Yes, it's ready. I don't know what you think you can gain by doing this, Schwab. We've already contacted several officials, including the federation attorney's office. You're just making matters worse for yourself. I am authorized to tell you that if you stop now, if you give yourself up before you leave this facility, the incident will be overlooked. No one has been hurt yet. We want to keep it that way. But if you proceed, especially if one man is mindwiped, I have orders to—"

"You won't be around to give them."

"There are standing orders to use deadly weapons and to use them on whatever scale is necessary to bring about your destruction."

"I'm going to the copter now. Remember what I said." Schwab broke the connection.

He finished the coffee—now cold—and started through the administration building toward the outer doors. He passed empty offices, his shoes echoing on the slick floors. He reached the outer doors and paused, looking through the thick plastic window. He could see a helicopter on the landing pad in front of the building, apparently an auto-piloted craft. He checked in both directions before pushing through the doors. At first trotting, then breaking into a sprint, he headed for the helicopter, afraid even to look back. If a dart hit him, he would rather not see it coming.

He left the sidewalk and started across the wide expanse of lawn. He expected any second to see ranks of men, all armed, appear from behind the helicopter or from around one of the buildings. None appeared. The helicopter, waiting, loomed up in front of him. Miraculously, he reached it, throwing open the door and clamoring into the plastic bubble. Immediately, he tapped the voice input to the helicopter's computer.

"Program through to Astra shuttleport—direct flight."

The helicopter responded instantly, lifting from the pad, hesitating a moment to change course, then starting its ascent to flight level. The prison facility dwindled to postage stamp size below him. Schwab glanced only briefly at the shrinking buildings. Instead, he found the emergency panel behind the seat and withdrew the tool kit, taking out several items and laying them on the passenger seat. He set to work on the controls.

Schwab knew the computer program would be automatically relayed to the prison facility and the local police, giving them his destination. The computerized air-traffic control for autopiloted craft would have been linked to the police computer before the helicopter was delivered to the prison administration building. The years of servicing and repairing starship computers gave Schwab a slight advantage. Once they were over the city, he would override the computer and take manual control, then divert the helicopter away from Astra shuttleport—the passenger terminal—to the freight shuttleport south of Los Angeles. It would at least give him a slight chance of evading capture.

After ten minutes flying time, Schwab had the jury-rigged manual override ready to engage. He let the helicopter begin its automatic approach to Astra. When he reached a level with more privately owned and individually operated helicopters than publicly owned and computer operated machines, he engaged the override. He hoped the unexpectedness of the act, causing his helicopter to disappear from the automatic tracking computer and re-appear as an anonymous privately operated blip—one to be avoided in the computer's automatic manipulation of its other helicopters—would happen too suddenly to let him be picked up by human observers.

The controls responded poorly, but at least they responded. For a fraction of a second, Schwab had envisioned the helicopter plummeting to the earth, uncontrollable by man or machine. Before changing course, Schwab brought the helicopter down to within a few meters of the ground. He knew the effort would have only minimal effect on any tracking radar but it might be enough. Flying low, hopping over residential areas, shopping centers and industrial parks, he arrived at the open fields surrounding the freight shuttleport.

Schwab circled the periphery of the shuttleport, carefully examining the wide low buildings, the men and equipment. Finally, on his second pass, he found what he wanted, a shuttle with Diversicorp markings on the flank.

He settled the helicopter onto the parking pad behind the building and popped open the door. Shuttleport noises burst into the quiet bubble: heavy equipment grinding in the distance, the clang of doors in the metal hangar building, the shouts of workmen.

Schwab stepped out onto the asphalt and started toward the hangar. A group of men stood near one door. One man was in the center, talking and giving orders, pointing in various directions as he assigned specific duties to each man. As the foreman gestured in Schwab's direction, his face became clear. Schwab recognized him, Phil Baroja, manager of the shuttle work crews.

Schwab hung back until the men had received their

orders. When the group around Baroja began to break up, Schwab stepped forward, catching the burly man's attention. Baroja—nearsighted—squinted, scrutinizing the beaconing figure. At last, he appeared startled as he recognized Schwab. He started talking as soon as Schwab was within earshot, yelling over the noise from the hangar.

"Ernie, what are you doing here? I thought they had you in—"

"They did. I have a big favor to ask you, Phil. I wouldn't do it if I could avoid it, but I can't. I don't have any choice."

Baroja waited, listening.

"I've just escaped from the federation holding facility. I—"

Baroja was almost physically stunned. The idea had obviously never occurred to him that Schwab was there for any other reason than having been released. "Escaped! I don't believe it! No one escapes from there!"

"I did."

"How?"

"That doesn't matter and I don't have time to explain it anyway. I need help, Phil. Without it, I go right back to that place and I'm not going back."

Baroja, still adjusting to the idea, stammered, "Ernie, this is preposterous. I can't remember anyone ever escaping from there. Why did they have you in there?"

The question reassured Schwab. Evidently, the reason for his arrest had not spread throughout the company. It might make things easier for him.

"They say I mindwiped the governor of a planet called Paria."

"Mind—"

"But I didn't—I mean, I did, but I didn't. It's complicated and I don't know all the answers. That's why I left there. I have to find out the answers. The only place I can find them is back on Paria. You'll just have to take my word that I'm not a criminal, telepathic or otherwise. If I can get back to Paria, I may be able to clear myself. I think I've come up with some information that may let me get at what really happened. Phil, you know me. Even if I could do something like that—and I can't, Phil, that's the hell of it—even if I could, would I?"

Baroja continued looking at Schwab, thinking, making up his mind. Finally, he nodded. "All right, Ernie. What do you want from me?"

"I want you to stow me away on a shuttle, then on a starship. Anything going even vaguely in the direction of Paria will do. I can make connections with other people once I'm in space."

"Ernie, if they catch either of us, it'll mean my job."

"I appreciate that, but if they catch me, it will mean a rehabilitation center. You know what they do to people in rehab centers. I'll come out a vegetable. I won't even be able to hold much of a job, much less get fired from one. Phil, this is my only chance. I've got to straighten things out. I must reach Paria as soon as possible."

Baroja hesitated a moment longer, as though making his final decision, then nodded. "Okay, Ernie, I'll see what I can do. Follow me."

"Okay, just a second. I have to get rid of that copter."

Schwab trotted back to the helicopter. He opened the door and reached under the control panel, detaching his jury-rigged manual override. He touched the return button on the console and stepped away from the machine. Slowly at first, then faster, the great blades began to turn. The helicopter lifted from the pad and moved upward at a steep angle. It would return to one of the numerous public helicopter stations, leaving little clue to its last stop.

Schwab returned to Baroja and followed him into the shuttle hangar. The gigantic bay doors on top of the shuttle were open, cranes loading in containerized cargo. As Schwab glanced up, one of the cranes was lifting a plastic crate the size of a small house and lowering it into the bay.

Baroja led Schwab under the tail of the shuttle and into an office area in the rear of the hangar. He told Schwab to wait, to talk to no one and if forced to talk, to say he was a new shuttle hand. "I'll be back as quickly as I can."

Schwab waited, five, ten, 15 minutes. At last, Baroja returned with a tall blond man wearing a shuttle pilot's uniform. Baroja introduced him as Allen Fausset, pilot of the shuttle being loaded in the hangar. Schwab was introduced as an impecunious relative of Baroja's who needed a ride up to the *Vercingétorix*, a starship orbiting Earth and destined for the quadrant containing Paria. The pilot, either indifferent to avoiding company regulations or willing to help Baroja—perhaps both—shook hands with Schwab and told him to wait until the cargo hold doors had closed. Baroja would supply Schwab with a set of crew's coveralls. When the cargo doors closed, Schwab was to watch for the crew and join them. Once inside the shuttle, Schwab was to stay out of the way until they reached orbit. At that point he could transfer to the starship.

Schwab thanked the man and watched him and Baroja leave. He waited in the office, glancing apprehensively from the shuttle bay doors to the crew's entrance to the hangar doors. So great was his anxiety that he almost failed to recognize the two policemen just inside the hangar.

CHAPTER 9

At first, he thought his own apprehension had suggested they were police. But the more he looked at them, the more certain he became of their true identity. Something about them, an aura, indicated their official status.

The two men began looking around the hangar for someone in authority. Finding no one, they began walking in the direction of the office.

Schwab looked quickly around the office. It offered few places to hide himself. He could think of only one alternative. If he could not disappear into the woodwork, he would have to blend in with it. He removed his coat, rolled up his sleeves and rumpled his hair slightly, then sat down behind Baroja's desk, picking up a cargo manifest and beginning to study it.

One of the two men remained outside the office when the other entered.

Schwab spoke to him without looking up. "Yeah, whatta you want?"

The man showed a federation law enforcement identification disk. Schwab gave it a perfunctory glance and returned his attention to the manifest, running the fingers of one hand through his hair and trying to block as much of his face as possible. He grunted at the identification disk. "So?"

"We're looking for a Diversicorp employee named Schwab, Mr. Baroja. We wondered if you could give us any information about him."

"Never heard of him," grunted Schwab. "I got work to

do. Will you guys get out of here and let me do it?"

"We won't take more than a few minutes of your time, sir."

"A few minutes too much."

"This man escaped from the federation detention facility here in Los Angeles."

Schwab grunted again. "Impossible."

"Until today, we would have agreed with you. He is a highly dangerous telepath. He has the capacity of completely and permanently emptying another man's mind at will. He cannot be allowed to remain at large."

Schwab turned a page on the cargo manifest, picking up a pencil and marking an item at random as though continuing work and annoyed at the officer's presence. "So catch him."

"That's the problem. We have to find him to catch him. We have reason to believe he may try to return to the scene of his crime, a place called Paria. He left the detention facility in a reaction copter. Somehow, he managed to make it disappear from the computer tracking system. We think he may turn to Diversicorp facilities in order to leave Earth."

Schwab inspected the manifest more closely, erasing a number, then printing it in again as if making a correction. "I don't know the man."

"If anyone strange shows up around here, will you please contact us? As I said, this man is extremely dangerous. We are getting out a bulletin on him at this very moment. I'll have one phonefaxed to you as soon as they're prepared."

"Fine, fine," said Schwab, his voice gruff. "Now get the hell out of here and let me get some work done."

The man hesitated a moment, as though about to add something, then left, closing the office door behind him. Schwab looked up to see the two men cross the hangar and exit through the main doors, two specks in the lower right-hand corner of a gigantic square of light.

Ten minutes later, Baroja returned with a set of coveralls for Schwab. Schwab donned them, and waiting for the great cargo doors to close on the shuttle, he wondered briefly about his experience with the police officer. The man had shown no sign of recognizing him. Either the deception, trying to appear as part of the shuttle service's working staff, or something else, had prevented the man making a connection. But what else? Schwab had lived nearly 30 years without ever recognizing his receptor telepath capacity. Perhaps he had other abilities, latent until called upon by necessity, waiting inside him to be used.

Schwab refused to let himself dwell on the thought and its implications—especially the implications. If other latent telepathic capacities existed in his makeup, perhaps one of them was responsible for his crime. Perhaps his entire pursuit for vindication was futile. Perhaps he would arrive on Paria and find nothing and no one responsible but himself.

Schwab pushed these considerations from his mind. First, he had to get to Paria. If the trip proved worthless, he would decide what to do then.

Schwab heard noise outside the office. He looked through the unpolarized windows at the shuttle. The cargo doors on its back had begun to close, the great panels sealing into a smooth, seamless line in the hull of the ship. The crew began filing out toward the craft.

"You'd better go, Ernie," said Baroja.

Schwab shook his friend's hand. "Phil, thank you for—"

Baroja waved aside the thanks. "Don't worry about it, Ernie. Now you'll owe me one."

Schwab left the office and caught up with the group approaching the shuttle. He fell in step behind the last man. Either Fausset had briefed them to expect Schwab—

or, at the least, to expect an additional crewman—or they accepted the sight of the coveralls as Schwab's authority to be with them. They nodded courteously but paid no further attention to him, continuing the walk to the escalator at the nose of the craft.

The crew filed onto the escalator and rode up the four-story height of the shuttle to the entrance port, disappearing inside one by one. When Schwab stepped through the port, he found Fausset waiting. Fausset nodded toward the rear of the shuttle, saying, "That way."

Schwab left the crew and found a place near the sealed lock to the cargo hold. He sat down and leaned the back of his head against the port to the hold. He could hear the forward port close. His ears popped as the cabin suddenly pressurized. At last, beginning to feel safe, Schwab let himself relax, the tension of the last few hours beginning to drain from him. He leaned against the bulkhead and closed his eyes a moment. He found it hard to believe that he was actually free at last.

Schwab felt only a slight movement as the shuttle was towed from the hangar. He felt even less during the lift-off. Once, he made his way to an observation port, thinking they would still be in the atmosphere. He was startled to discover only the black of space and the sharp pinpoint of stars. In the distance, gradually enlarging, he could see the *Vercingétorix*, its bulbous command center trailing three parallel tubes, the passenger, cargo and crew compartments. At least Schwab would eat well. The *Vercingétorix* had a fine reputation within Diversicorp for the quality of its food.

HALF an hour later, Schwab found himself aboard the starship. Fausset had arranged for his transfer with a smoothness that amounted to slight-of-hand. The shuttle captain had spoken to friends in the starship crew and even arranged a birth for Schwab. By the time the starship broke orbit and started its acceleration run out of the solar system, even Schwab was beginning to marvel at how far he had gone.

During the first day of acceleration as the ship prepared to reach half-light speed before it shifted into hyperspace, Schwab felt reluctant to leave his cabin. Finally, with only a few hours to go before he would have to take up a position on the suspended animation couch, he decided to put in an appearance in the passenger lounge. The chance of being recognized was small. Yet his failure to mingle with the other passengers might be remarked upon as peculiar.

He made his way to the lounge. Shortly before the shift to hyperspace, the passenger lounge of any starship was always full. Passengers like to exchange information about destinations and make friends. The small space set aside for the lounge doubled as the dining room. A long table of cold cuts was laid out against one wall. Schwab walked to it and put together a sandwich. He was about to begin eating the sandwich when a quarrel erupted near the doorway, a short man with a red face gesturing and shouting up at a sober and impassive ship's officer. By straining, Schwab could catch a few of the words.

". . . Escaped! . . . Utterly incredible! . . . why wasn't I notified immediately?"

The ship's officer tried to answer.

The red-faced man cut him off. "Incompetence! Gross and willful incompetence!"

"Governor Finnley—" began the officer.

". . . should have been notified hours ago!"

Some passengers near Schwab began talking, drowning out the argument across the room. Schwab returned to his sandwich. As he took his second bite, the red-faced man, Finnley, abruptly turned away from the officer and started across the room toward the cold cuts, muttering to himself as he walked.

He reached the table and began slapping cold cuts onto

a slice of bread, working his way down the table and talking to himself. ". . . gross incompetence . . . man's out of the cage four hours and no one tells me . . . ought to have the whole lot of them drummed out of the service. . . ."

Finnley arrived at the end of the table, slapped a second piece of bread on his creation and looked around for something to drink.

"There's coffee in those taps," said Schwab.

"Ah, thank you. At least somebody's doing something right."

Finnley got a cup of coffee and took up a position next to Schwab.

Schwab took another bite of his own sandwich. "I couldn't help overhearing some of your conversation with the communications officer."

"Communications officer," snorted Finnley. "So that's who he thought he was." Finnley glanced up at Schwab, scrutinizing his face a moment as if deciding whether to reveal a confidence. "The way the man blurted out everything, I don't suppose you failed to get the subject of our conversation."

"Evidently, someone failed to notify you of something."

"If that were all it was, I would have expected it. I have noticed in the course of my career that there are people who do not go out of their way to notify me of things. No, no, Mr.—?"

"Sch . . . Schulman," said Schwab.

"My name's Finnley, Charles C. Finnley." They shook hands. "No, it is the content of this communication that is distressing me."

He stared at Schwab and said abruptly, "Have you ever heard of a planet called Paria?"

"Yes."

Finnley's eyebrows went up. "Yes? That's odd. I'd never heard of it until a few weeks ago."

"I'm a starship hand."

"On this ship?"

"No, I'm deadheading to Wolff-72-3."

Finnley grunted, satisfied, disinterested. "I have been appointed governor of that godforsaken world. It is, as I understand from my background briefing, a desolate and uninteresting place—frankly, the last gasp in my fading career."

"I should think being appointed governor—"

"Is fine for someone on his way up—someone like Jeremy Morris." Finnley spit out the name. "But for someone like me, it is an insult. I am 53 years old, Mr. Schulman, 53. The fact that they have given me this pockmarked world in the middle of nowhere—in fact, not even the entire planet, just the human concession—to govern, that fact alone shows that someone lacks the proper confidence in my abilities."

Schwab murmured something appropriately sympathetic.

"Yes, yes," said Finnley. "You and I might feel that way, but they don't. Still, if I handle things well on Paria—unlike the late governor of that rat-hole world—my next appointment might be closer to Earth, possibly even on Earth itself." Finnley smiled a moment, contemplating it. "Earth—what I wouldn't give for a complete tour of service there. I have been on these deadend planets so long I can hardly remember what Earth is like."

"Didn't you just come from there?"

Finnley's smile disappeared. "Yes. Three whole days I was given, then here I am, back in harness, heading for this nowhere world in the center of . . . of. . . ."

"Nowhere," suggested Schwab.

"Exactly. And what is the first thing that happens to me in this new position?"

Schwab shook his head. "I don't know. What?"

"Some mindwiping telepath—the very telepath who got

rid of my late and not-very-lamented predecessor—escapes from the maximum security facility at Los Angeles. Have you ever seen that place?"

"I saw it once from the air."

"The place is impregnable—from inside or out. Yet this creature escapes from it. And how?"

"How?"

"He threatens to mindwipe everyone in the place unless he is let out, so they do it—for heaven's sake. Just let him walk right out scot-free. It is utterly beyond my comprehension. But then, that is always the weak link in the system, isn't it, Mr. Schulman?"

Schwab momentarily felt he had missed some essential part of the conversation. "What's the weak link?"

"People!" said Finnley triumphantly. "People are the weakest link in any system. Here is this perfectly good prison that not even the Count of Monte Cristo himself could escape from and this mad mindwiper walks right out as though they handed him the keys. It is utterly disgusting. Then what do they do—the ignoramuses?"

"I'd be interested to hear."

"I'm certain you would. I hope you write your federation senator about it. Gross inefficiency! Gross!"

Finnley settled down to glowering and mumbling.

Schwab tried to prod more information out of the man. "Then what did they do?"

"Oh, yes. They forget to inform me of what they did! I am going to govern the very colony this mindwiper preyed upon—to govern from the very office in which the deed occurred—and they tell me nothing of this vicious beast's escape until it is too late!"

"Too late for what?"

"Anything, my dear Mr. Schulman, anything!"

"I'm sure he'll be apprehended soon enough."

"I'm not. With the gross incompetence shown so far, the creature could be on this very ship for all we know."

"I doubt that. It seems to me someone in his position—fleeing the authorities—would have a difficult time leaving Earth."

Slightly mollified, Finnley nodded. "Perhaps. Still, they always return to the scene of their crimes."

"Telepaths?"

"Criminals."

"So I've heard."

"Sometimes," said Finnley, great weariness in his voice, "I think they have devised it all to test me."

"Who?"

"They! The Sector Coordinator. Maybe even higher than that! The Quadrant Chamberlain or even the Federation Colonial Undersecretary himself! They want to know what I'm made of." Finnley's face took on a look of grim resolution. "I will show them what I'm made of. If this telepathic beast shows up on my colony, I shall—" Finnley made a gesture as though wringing out a washcloth "—exterminate him."

On the opposite side of the lounge, a large red sign lit, accompanied by a loud chime. The sign instructed passengers to return to their cabins in preparation for insertion into suspended animation couches and the shift to hyperspace.

He pointed out the sign to Finnley, who grunted. They shook hands again and parted, Finnley thanking Schwab for supplying a sympathetic ear.

Schwab smiled. "It was a pleasure, Governor Finnley. Perhaps I'll see you again if I ever get to Paria."

"I certainly hope so, Mr. Schulman. You'll have no trouble finding me. It is—" Finnley glowered. "—a small colony."

Schwab returned to his cabin. He could have prepared the suspended animation couch himself. He had done so numerous times during his years in space. But he decided to wait for his cabin steward. It might not pay to seem too familiar with ship's operations. He had no idea what story Fausset had given the man.

The steward arrived shortly. Quickly, efficiently, he lifted the plastic bubble over the suspended animation couch and helped Schwab lie down. Every time Schwab prepared for a hyperspace jump, he had a feeling of vulnerability. Having to rely completely on automatic equipment for life support, with no possibility of repairing the equipment if something failed, always bothered him.

The steward stood above him, holding the long plastic blister and preparing to close it. He was giving his standard speech on the suspended animation couch, one he probably delivered at least ten times before he went to his own couch. ". . . and if there is any equipment failure, you will be immediately revived. If the failure in any way involves the life-support system outside the couch, you will not be able to raise—" the steward nodded toward the blister "—this cover. That is, of course, for your own protection. Computer warnings will be flashed on the cover in front of your eyes. You will have to wait either for automatic release or for one of the crew to come and release you manually. In the event such a thing occurs—and I might add it has never occurred on any Diversicorp ship during the seven years of my service. . . ."

Schwab remembered a systems failure on the *Reynard*, the first starship he served in, but said nothing.

The steward continued. "If such a thing should happen, don't panic. We have adequate safeguard procedures. Do you understand?"

Schwab nodded.

"Good, sir. One last thing. We have a complete library of memory tapes. Though your metabolism is slowed considerably during suspended animation, it is not completely stopped. I can arrange to have a tape on any subject that might interest you fed into your unconscious mind. Do you have any preference?"

Schwab thought a moment. "I'm going to a place called Paria. I believe it's a somewhat out-of-the-way place. If you have anything about the planet, I would appreciate knowing it."

"Certainly, sir. I'll check the library." The steward began closing the bubble. "Pleasant dreams, sir."

The cover clicked into place around Schwab. Through the plastic, he saw the steward touch a series of numbers on a small computer display near the couch. Faintly, he heard the hiss of the gas. The faint taste, unique and almost imperceptible, reassured him. Its scent was nothing like the knockout gas at the prison.

Schwab inhaled deeply, feeling himself relax. Gradually, his eyes closed. He shivered once, feeling the first level of cryogenic cooling. Cold was always the worst part of suspended animation, especially when waking up.

Schwab inhaled again and all became blackness.

REGINA

He *will be back soon. I have counted the days. He said he would only be gone a short time. It is not him that I really want. It is what he brings me. I am tired of eating synthetic food. I want real food. He will also bring me new animals for my collection. I will like that. I do not care what they are as long as they are new. I am even beginning to tire of my old animals. For a long time, I have been tired of the ugly computers. They are his, not mine. I have never liked them. Yet, we must use them. If men are to be what we want them to be, we must use them. Some day, they will no longer be necessary. Some day, the evil in men will be gone. Some day, men will thank us for what we are doing. They will love us. They will love me.*

CHAPTER 10

" . . . *Malfunction couch twenty-seven* . . . *malfunction couch twenty-seven* . . . *malfunction couch twenty-seven* . . . "

The words sounded hollow and distant in Benson's ears. He tried to concentrate on them. Malfunction . . . couch . . . something . . . something. He tried to listen. He tried to make the words mean something. His eyes flickered open momentarily. Before them, projected in large red letters on the plastic blister of the suspended animation couch, the words appeared again.

MALFUNCTION—EVACUATE COUCH—
MALFUNCTION.

Behind the lettering, he could see vague shapes moving, distorted images faintly like men. One shape reached toward the other, passing a large blurry object to the second shape.

Benson's eyes closed. He could make no sense of the scene. Slowly, gradually, he became aware of his body. It was cold—freezing. He felt his limbs begin to tremble, his teeth chatter. His mind groping, he began to realize he was dying. The couch had malfunctioned on the revival cycle. If it had malfunctioned before revival, he would have already been dead.

Benson tried to move. The pain was excruciating. Every limb felt numb and made of pain. Even his heart, its beat gradually increasing, sent surges of pain through his chest. Focusing all his attention on the red numbers before his eyes, trying—unsuccessfully—to ignore the pain, Benson reached up and began pushing on the plastic blister, the agony increasing the more force he exerted.

The shapes on the other side of the plastic went into a flurry of soundless activity, working desperately over the couch. Benson continued pushing, feeling his consciousness dwindle the longer he exerted himself. Then, suddenly, the plastic blister gave under his push and sprang open. Hands reached out and grabbed him, their touch adding to the torture he had already caused himself. He was being lifted and transferred to a gurney. Someone said something in a reassuring tone. The gurney began to move. Benson lost consciousness.

Later, he revived in the starship's sick bay.

A doctor, her back to Benson, heard him move and turned around. "Ah, Mr. Benson, you're awake. Good. I was about to give you a stimulant. We won't need that now."

"What happened?"

"Couch malfunction."

"I realize that. What caused it?"

"They're still checking the systems. It was something in the revival cycle. Frankly, Mr. Benson, you are a lucky man. In my personal experience, I have never seen a couch fail. I checked the literature as soon as I knew of it. In most of the cases—and, by the way, 95 percent of them were during the early years of interstellar travel—the result was either death or permanent cell damage, especially to the nervous system and brain. Why did you push against the blister?"

Benson shrugged. "Instinctive, probably. Did it help?"

The doctor smiled. "Not as you intended. I'm told it did very little, if anything, toward opening the blister, other than stimulate the work crew to move faster. It did, however, increase your circulation. Without it, you might have suffered substantial brain damage."

"Then there was some damage."

"Not that I can detect. I do want to keep you here until we rendezvous with the *Reynard* and you transfer to the last leg of your journey. That should be in a day or two. If there's anything you want—"

"I'd like to know the cause of the malfunction as soon as *they* do."

The doctor lifted one eyebrow, her smile showing at the same time. "Morbid curiosity?"

"Professional curiosity."

The doctor showed Benson how to channel in magazine tapes from the ship's library and left, saying she would be back from time to time to check on his condition.

Benson spent the next day and a half in bed, recuperating. He marked his progress by how he felt on his trips to the bathroom. Each time, his legs became steadier, his balance more assured. On the morning of the second day, the sick bay door slid back and Cowdin peered in.

The engineer saw Benson, smiled and approached. He stopped next to the bed. "You're looking well, Mr. Benson."

"I feel better," answered Benson. "Except for this damn cold. Even a suspended animation couch malfunction didn't get rid of it."

Cowdin smiled. "I'm glad to see that you're better. I was shocked to hear about the accident, needless to say. If I were you, I'd see a lawyer."

Benson nodded agreement but kept himself from smiling. "I did have a few ideas along that line. What can I do for you, Mr. Cowdin?"

"My primary purpose in visiting you, of course, is to ask about your health. I see it's improving."

"But you had a secondary purpose."

"Only to renew my offer of assistance. I may be able to help you conduct your business on Paria in spite of the fact that you'll probably be returning to Earth with this ship. I do know most of the important people in the colony and—"

Benson let his face show some surprise. "Returning to Earth? Where did you—"

Cowdin looked flustered. "But your condition—"

"Is, I'm told, satisfactory. According to the ship's doctor—"

A voice interrupted from the door to the sick bay. "According to me, he can leave us any time he wants to and continue his journey to any destination."

The doctor approached. Benson introduced her to Cowdin.

Cowdin's face acquired a look of grave concern. "But surely, Doctor, the metabolic damage—"

"Was slight enough to be negligible. I'm happy to say my patient can give me back that diagnostic bed any time he pleases."

Benson smiled and began to get up, throwing back the covers.

Cowdin, momentarily disconcerted, at last smiled, nodding to Benson. "Well, that's good to hear. As I said before, Mr. Benson, please don't hesitate to call on my services when you reach Paria."

"Thank you," said Benson.

Cowdin left.

Benson, his eyes lingering on the sick-bay door, spoke to the doctor. "You don't happen to know when Mr. Cowdin was brought out of suspended animation, do you?"

"No, but I can find out. By the way, they did isolate the cause of your couch failure."

"And?"

"The manual override circuits had somehow been crossed with the automatic equipment. Each system was countermanding the other's orders halfway through the revival cycle."

"How did that happen?"

The doctor shrugged. "No one knows. The best guess is a defective circuit. They do, occasionally, wear out."

"You said the manual override circuit. Does that mean someone could have had physical access to it?"

"I suppose so. Why?"

Benson continued looking at the door. "Nothing. Just a thought.'

Benson was up and around with sufficient time to pack and make the transfer to the *Reynard*, the sister ship of Schwab's own *Chanticleer*. The transfer itself, accomplished after the two ships docked in space, required him only to walk through a short passage to the second ship. Aboard the *Reynard*, a star-class freighter, the passenger accommodations were rudimentary compared with the more lavish passenger liner. Still, they were adequate. The last day and a half of the trip was uneventful. Benson, using the excuse of his accident, stayed in his cabin. Actually, he wanted to avoid Cowdin and any further offers of help.

Benson used the ship's library to read up o Paria. As McMasters had said, the planet revolved around an F spectra star. Earth, by comparison, revolved around a G spectra star. Other than the visual effect of dullness that Benson had already noticed on the kineticorder tape, the difference in star types had little effect on the planet's habitability. Due to the sporadic vegetation on Paria, the oxygen-nitrogen-ozone balance was slightly different than Earth's, but again habitable.

The human colony had been located in the least interesting spot on the planet, an arid plain with nothing but the Parian mounds to break the monotony. From what Benson had seen on the tape, the mounds actually added to the monotony rather than relieved it. The planet's mining activities dictated the colony's location and also provided the reason for its existence. Without pyraclore ore, men would never have settled on the planet. If the center of human activity had been put near the more accommodating areas of vegetation, the logistics of transferring the ore dug out of the planet by the Parians to the place for transfer to a shuttle would have become unnecessarily complicated. In short, reflected Benson, Paria was as dull as its sunlight.

At the end of the second day, the starship reached Paria, taking up a synchronized parking orbit over the human colony. Benson was notified when a shuttle had been prepared. He had asked for a printout in the ship's library of an article on the Parians themselves. He took it with him to the shuttle, hoping to use it to avoid conversation with Cowdin. The ruse proved unnecessary: Cowdin sat at the far end of the shuttle, absorbed in papers of his own.

When the great doors in the side of the *Reynard* parted to eject the shuttle, Benson hardly noticed. He felt a slight change in the shuttlecraft's attitude when the photon auxiliary engines fired to slow their descent toward Paria. Aside from that, he remembered little of the journey to the surface. Instead, he read the scant information in the article on the Parians. They were classified as intelligent creatures for legal purposes, i.e., any dealings with them had to conform to the Federation Code sections relating to commerce between sentient beings, not as between master and slave or owner and chattel. Beyond that, the rat-bodied creatures had been little studied. Some xenobiologists guessed that the tunneling and mound building of the creatures had as much religious significance as practical meaning. No one speculated on the intrinsic meaning, the substance of the creature's beliefs.

Benson's first awareness of the landing came when the gyros were cut out. The entire passenger compartment moved slightly, then the door slid back, letting in the dull sunlight Benson had expected. Cowdin, closer to the exit, left first, followed by several crewmen from the *Reynard*. Benson found himself the last to exit.

He stepped out onto the shuttleside stairs and blinked against the sunlight. At the foot of the stairs, he saw someone familiar, Curly Curtis, waving to him. Benson descended the stairs and shook hands with Curly.

"I've got a dustrover over here, Mr. Benson. I'll take you to the hotel."

"To what do I owe this red carpet treatment?"

Curly laughed. "Hardly red carpet, but it's better than walking." They reached the dustrover. "Hop in. We can talk on the way."

The two men climbed into the dustrove Curly driving. Once the machine was under way, its great tires lurching over the uneven ground while the body of the vehicle remained level, Curly asked about Schwab.

"The last time I saw him," said Benson, "he was doing just fine—depressed, but surviving."

"When I heard you were coming to Paria, I figured you had something that might help Ernie. Do you?"

"I don't know. Maybe."

"You wouldn't want to tell me what it is?"

"No."

"Maybe I can help."

"What do you know about a man named Cowdin?"

Curly shrugged. "Not much. He's been here as long as anyone—except Max Jacobson, of course. He keeps to himself and runs our mining operation and the liaison with the critters. I'm mostly involved in ore transfer so I don't see too much of him. Indirectly, I suppose, he's my boss here, but I never see him in the warehouses."

"Who's Max Jacobson?"

Curly gave a broad grin. "Our local eccentric, our founder actually. He's been here since before there was a here. He's the third force in local politics, if a place this size can be said to have politics. The government, Diversicorp and Max Jacobson. Tough old buzzard. Doesn't take any lip from Cowdin or our people in Diversicorp, or from the government. I remember one time they assigned me—" One wheel of the dustrover hit a chuckhole, unexpectedly tossing Benson and his suitcases slightly into the air. Curly glanced at him. "You okay?"

Benson nodded. "Fine. Go on."

"Sorry about that. After a couple of months in this place, you get used to chuckholes. You never know when one's going to pop up in front of you. They move around, shift like sand dunes. They tell me it has to do with the critters digging down there. One day the road'll be full of them, the next it's smooth as a rug. Anyway, what was I talking about?"

"Max Jacobson."

"Oh, yeah, Max. So they assigned me to go along with one of the government men while the guy tried to collect a hotel tax from Max. I thought it was a little strange being assigned to do government duty when Diversicorp was paying my salary, but I was new here. We double up all the time. During big ore shipments, I've seen government clerks handle cranes like pros. Anyway, we went up to Max armed with this tax bill from Governor Cassell—" Curly glanced at Benson, simultaneously letting the dustrover bounce through another chuckhole. "That was Morris's predecessor, a horrible governor. Corrupt as the day is long—and here that's about 30-odd hours. Old Cassell finally made enough money off us poor slobs to retire on Earth. He's got a big place near Mumbwa in Africa, I hear. Anyway, he's the one who sent us to Max with this tax bill. Max took one look at it and went through the roof. What did we mean by '*All* hotels on Paria are subject to the tax'? We knew as well as anyone that there weren't any other hotels on Paria. Therefore, since he had no intention of paying some fabricated tax that would go directly into

Cassell's pocket, none of the hotels on Paria were going to pay the tax. I tried to reason with him."

"No doubt that was a mistake."

"A big one. He just got angrier. I tried to point out that he could pass the tax along to his customers, that it didn't actually come out of his pocket. Max wanted none of it. He said if Cassell wanted the tax collected he could walk from his office himself and collect it. He also allowed as to how if he saw Cassell's face in any way but socially—that is, if Cassell actually tried to collect the tax—the rent on Cassell's private residence apartment would be tripled, which meant it would exceed the federation housing allotment and come directly out of Cassell's pocket."

"What did Cassell have to say about that?"

"He just shrugged it off and said it had been worth a try. I think he finally instituted a landing tax to make up what he lost on Max. Anyway, the point is, Max doesn't take much guff from anyone. He was here before anyone else and he feels like the American Indians must have felt, that their land had been taken away from them but eventually they would get it back. There's about as much chance of that happening with Max as there was with the Indians."

Benson tried but failed to remember paying any landing tax. He mentioned the fact to Curly.

Curly shrugged. "That was Morris's doing. After Cassell cleared out, they stuck Morris in here. He was trying to clean things up before—" Curly hesitated "—before it happened."

Curly noticed Benson's lack of reaction and continued. "Damn shame, bright young fellow like Morris. He was making good headway on turning this colony into something worth living in—at least in terms of the human population. Those giant rodents and this—" Curly gestured around at the passing landscape, dry and barren "—Sahara ain't never going to bloom. But I will say this much for Morris, he stuck his nose in everywhere and if things weren't right, he did something about it."

The dustrover penetrated the static field outside the concession. Immediately the ride became smoother, the even surface of the road within the static field kept intact by the lack of too disruptive a wind and frequent maintainence. Curly turned left at the first—almost the only—corner and skidded the dustrover to a halt in front of the hotel. Benson got out and lifted his suitcases from the back seat.

Curly sat a moment watching Benson, his face indicating he wanted to ask a question but felt reluctant to do so. Benson thanked Curly for the ride.

"No big thing. If you need any other help, give me a call."

"Where can I find this Max Jacobson of yours?"

Curly nodded toward the hotel. "In there, if he's in the concession at all. He likes to go out and commune with nature. At least that's what he calls it. How you can commune with this place I don't know. If he isn't there, you'll probably find Eldridge."

"Who's Eldridge?"

"Max's nephew. Max works him to death for peanuts and claims he's teaching the boy a trade. No, I take that back. Max tries to work him to death. Eldridge has too many of Max's traits to let it happen." Curly grinned. "You'll see what I mean when you meet him."

Benson thanked Curly again and walked toward the hotel steps.

"Mr. Benson."

Benson stopped and glanced around. "Yes?"

"What do you think Ernie's chances are?"

"Curly, I really don't know. That's what I'm here to find out."

CHAPTER 11

At least, thought Benson observing the empty lobby, out of the way places had the advantage of not having line-ups. He carried his suitcases to the desk and lowered them to the floor. After several minutes of waiting, he dinged a small, old-fashioned hotel bell on the counter.

No one responded.

He dinged it again.

Still no answer.

"Hey! Anyone home?"

Slowly, a door opened at one end of the lobby. A young man emerged, doing what Benson could only describe as a slow motion lope across the lobby. Eventually, the young man arrived at the desk, lifted an insert in the counter and stepped through. He approached Benson from the other side of the counter. "Can I help you?"

"I'd like a room."

"I guessed that much."

"It shows, does it?"

"Anytime I see someone I don't know in here, I usually figure they want a room. Sometimes it shows. Sometimes it doesn't. In your case, it's a toss-up. But they all want a room. This is the only hotel around, so it figures."

Benson, slightly taken aback by the man's attitude, nodded. "Yes, it figures. Can I have a room?"

"You want southern, northern, eastern or western exposure?"

"Does it matter?"

"Nope."

"Then why ask?"

"Courtesy. My uncle's big on courtesy."

"Your uncle's Max Jacobson."

"He was the last time I looked. But you never know about him."

"I'd like to talk to him."

"About what?"

"Business."

Eldridge grunted. "Any business you got with him you can take up with me. What I'm doing here, they tell me, is learning the business."

"I'd rather talk to your uncle."

"You can't."

"I can't? You mean you're not going to let me?"

"I mean he's not here. Hasn't been for a week. The old crow's off communing with what he likes to call 'nature.' When he gets back, I'll tell him you asked for him, Mr.—" Eldridge waited, eyebrows lifted, expecting a response of some kind from Benson.

Benson gestured at the hotel register, again an old-fashioned book instead of the usual computer link to a credit checking service. The clerk moved the register into position in front of Benson, spinning it to face him and offering a pen. Benson signed. Eldridge spun the register around and looked at the name, grunting once.

Benson returned the pen. "I take it you're Eldridge Jacobson."

"That's me, Max's slave, lackey, coolie and nephew. Most of the time, it's one of the first three. Since Max has been gone, I'm beginning to feel a little less like the first three and a little more like the last."

"Max is hard to work for."

"Are Parians hard to cook?"

The reference threw Benson for a moment. "I take it they are."

"Don't ask me. Ask Max. He's the only one I know

who's ever eaten one. It was, by the way, back in the old days before the Parians came under federation protection. It's against the law to eat intelligent creatures, you know."

"So I've heard. Did your uncle say what they tasted like?"

"It seems to change every time he tells the story. Sometimes it's bear, sometimes it's chicken. I've never been able to pin him down on it. He always changes the subject and starts talking about the old days in general and how wonderful this dump was before humanity showed up. Max considers anything over half a dozen people humanity."

Eldridge snatched a key off a peg behind him and lifted the movable section of the counter, stepping into the lobby and directing Benson toward the stairs. As he lead Benson down a corridor to his room, Eldridge glanced at him.

"You don't look like you're with the government. Are you?"

"No."

"Didn't think so. Most of those guys look like they're frightened of their own shadow, especially nowadays after the mindwiping we had. You hear about that?"

Benson nodded.

"You don't look like Diversicorp either."

"Glad to hear it."

They reached a corner room on the second floor. Eldridge halted, about to open the door but hesitating and glancing at Benson. "What I'm getting at in my obviously too subtle way is what you're doing on Paria."

"Minding my own business."

Instead of a hostile reaction, Eldridge laughed. "That I don't believe. You don't look like the type who does that either."

"What type do I look like?"

Eldridge considered Benson, head canted slightly, one eye almost closed. "If I didn't know better—since we never get any on Paria—I'd say you were a lawyer."

"Close."

Eldridge opened the door and led Benson into the room. Benson felt a sudden sensation of *déjà vu*. He had seen the room before, on Schwab's kineticorder tape. It was the room Schwab had been given on his short visit to Paria.

"This," said Eldridge, after giving Benson an opportunity to look around the room, "is what we call our celebrity suite. In this very room slept the telepath who mindwiped our late governor. Other than being the only hotel on the planet—therefore, the best—that is our single claim to fame. Max wanted to put up a sign. I told him some of the government people might be offended." Eldridge handed Benson the key and started for the door, evidently not expecting a tip. "I'm sure you'll enjoy telling your friends back home about it. You can take pictures if you like."

Eldridge left, slamming the door.

Benson spent the next day and a half learning about the human colony on Paria, its geography, unimpressive and miniscule, its social structure, equally divided between federation and Diversicorp personnel, and its politics. On this last point, he expected to find little of interest. A lengthy conversation with Eldridge Jacobson, plus discussions with both federation and Diversicorp personnel in the hotel bar, proved him wrong. Where humans lived together in a community, there were politics. The crux of Paria's human politics had to do with Diversicorp's mining operations or, more exactly, with the miners.

The Parians, asserted the Diversicorp-dominated faction—though some federation personnel adhered to the view—would dig their tunnels with its valuable by-product whether human beings were present on the planet to take advantage of it or not. With the human presence, the Parians received the benefits of human technology to aid them in something they would do anyway. In exchange, mankind obtained large quantities of pyraclore ore.

The second faction, dominated by federation government personnel and at one time led by Governor Morris, contended the arrangement left the Parians in a forever servile position. Because the creatures would become more and more dependent on human technology, they would have less of a chance to develop their own technical culture. Most of Morris's efforts during the last months of his governorship were directed toward banning human activity on Paria. Morris's main difficulty in achieving his goal was in trying to convince the higher levels of federation bureaucracy that the Parians indeed had potential to go beyond their current cultural level. At the time of his mindwiping, he was said to have been developing a complete profile of the Parian culture for presentation to the Federation Colonial Administration office.

Benson found these conversations enlightening. They provided a potential motive for someone other than Schwab, who had no motive, to want Morris removed. Still, even though it gave Benson something like a working thesis for his continued investigations, there were no specific answers to his most important questions—who and how. He decided the best approach would be to talk to everyone of importance on the planet. He had already, briefly, talked to Cowdin. Morris's replacement, someone named Finnley, was due the following day. That left Max Jacobson, who returned to the hotel from his communing with nature on the afternoon of Benson's second day on Paria.

Benson had decided to go downstairs to the hotel bar for lunch. He arrived in the lobby in time to see Eldridge being chewed out by an old man with a backpack, a long walking stick and a beard down to his belt. Benson stood at the base of the stairs a moment, listening to the one-sided discussion. The old man was ticking off points on his fingers, stating the point, holding up a finger, stating another point and adding another finger.

". . . and thirdly—" a third finger joined two already in the air "—where the hell is the rent check from those bureaucratic bunglers on the third floor? I want you to remember this, Eldridge. This hotel does not extend credit to anyone, even the so-called Federation of United Worlds. They can go bankrupt just like anyone else—then where would we be? I ask you that?"

"Uncle Max—"

"And fourthly—" a fourth finger joined the three aloft. "—why does the kitchen look like a giant Aldebran cockroach has been sleeping there all night?"

"I haven't had a chance to—"

"Make the chance, you worthless sack of dust and bones! Make the chance!" The great head shook slowly, moving the beard back and forth across the chest. "When my brother convinced me you were the right one to take on here as an assistant, I thought I was getting a bargain—a relative, someone who would at least care enough about the place to keep the giant cockroaches out of the kitchen—"

"Uncle Max, there are no cockroaches—giant or otherwise—in the kitchen."

"That's what you say, but you haven't been in there in so long you wouldn't know if there was a Parian squatting in each corner. I was wrong when I said yes to your father. You aren't worth the price it would cost me to have you shipped out of here, lock, stock and insolent manners. Eldridge, you are undoubtedly the worst employee I have ever had in this hotel."

"Uncle Max, I'm the only employee you've ever had."

"That's beside the point. I never intend to have another one—that's for certain—especially if they turn out like you—lazy, worthless, good for nothing."

"Are you finished, Uncle Max?"

"No, I'm not finished." Behind the red beard the face

was scarlet, an almost healthy color even in the Parian light. "Do I look finished?"

Eldridge ignored the question and nodded toward Benson. "I think our new guest wants to talk to you, Uncle Max."

The bearded man whirled on Benson, gave him a furious look up and down, then fixed his stare on Benson's eyes, frowning. "What about?"

Benson walked across the lobby and introduced himself. Max Jacobson's large hand enveloped Benson's. As soon as Benson mentioned Schwab's name, Jacobson shook his head.

"Don't know anything about it, Benson. The man was a complete stranger to me. Never saw him before. Hope I never see him again. In fact, I didn't even see him at all." Jacobson jerked a thumb toward Eldridge. "Dumb-dumb here checked him in. The man was a stranger, pure and simple. I think he was one of that lot that goes around despoiling the landscape. You might check with them."

"You mean Diversicorp."

Jacobson's face took on a look of mock surprise. "You mean there's more?"

"Not that I know of."

"Good. There's one too many right now. All I know about it I heard from the boy here. Sounds like a typical example of his poor judgment. You'd think, living around me, he would pick up a few good habits, wouldn't you? Does he? Hell no! Lets anyone and everyone come into this hotel—despoilers, government types, mindwipers, even—what do you do?"

"I'm a lawyer."

"Even lawyers. The boy's got no sense about things like that."

Benson, slightly annoyed, returned Jacobson's gaze. "I'm sure you've been told you have a winning personality."

Jacobson snorted. "What the hell do I need with a win ning personality?" Jacobson gestured around at the lobby with his walking stick. "I own the damn hotel! Only hotel on the planet. People either do business with me or they sleep on the ground. I need a winning personality like I need a hole in the head. I got 'em all by the tail." Jacob son's expression changed, becoming a scowl. "Everyone except this lazy nephew of mine. Have you ever seen any body as lazy as this? I'm gone a week and the entire hotel falls apart. I can imagine what it'll come to when I kick off." Jacobson waved the walking stick around again, indicating the hotel. "Dust! Dust! Dust! It'll reclaim every thing. Nobody'll know how to survive out here."

Eldridge Jacobson, a look of extreme exasperation on his face, glanced at Benson. "My uncle exaggerates."

Max Jacobson snorted, ignoring Eldridge and glaring at Benson. "Everything they know, they learned from me, Bunson. People like me come out here in one-man scout ships, bringing nothing but our knuckles and a Bowie knife—"

"And the latest in one-man exploration equipment," added Eldridge.

"Shut up, Eldridge. I'm talking to this man."

"You're talking at him, Uncle Max."

"Yes, Bursons," said Jacobson, his tone of voice be coming reflective, "that's what they all think. They think we had the best of equipment. We had nothing, I tell you, nothing! Why, when I landed here the first time, this place was as bare and empty as my nephew's brain. Yessir. I had to fight the Parians for every centimeter of ground I got. I had to fight them tooth and nail—"

"Knuckle and Bowie knife," interjected Eldridge.

"Damn right!" Jacobson reached out and rebounded his fist from Benson's shoulder, causing Benson to sway back ward slightly. "I like you, Bentsword. I can see you're my kind of man. I can see if we were out here in the old days,

ve would have fought it out together, sometimes back to
back, sometimes face to face."

"Like a dance," sighed Eldridge.

"Exactly. Hell of a dance it would have been, too. Why,
Bluntsword, I remember one time I got trapped in the
tunnels and had to cut my way out through those Parian
devils."

"I wasn't aware the Parians were aggressive creatures,"
said Benson.

"Shows what you know, doesn't it? You've probably
been reading that tripe Cowdin tries to pass off on people
as scholarship, but them critters are mean, Brownsword,
mean! You catch 'em in the wrong mood and they'll gob-
ble you up—" Jacobson snapped his fingers "— quick as
that."

Listening to Jacobson, Benson's attention had at first
wandered. Then he began to listen more closely. So much
of the man's attitude struck Benson as a pose, a stance
Jacobson put on for the world, that he found it hard to
believe Jacobson actually believed what he was saying.
Benson had seen the same thing happen in court, people
adopting an attitude they thought would be convincing.
Under it, he usually found something more interesting
than the pose. He decided to turn Max Jacobson's conversation slightly, hoping to get behind the frontiersman
pose.

"Mr. Jacobson, you seem to be less than fond of what
civilization has brought to Paria."

"Dead set against it! Despoilers—that's all your civilization brought! Not one of 'em's worth half of Eldridge over
here—" Eldridge smiled at this first word of praise from
his uncle "—and Eldridge isn't worth a monkey's uncle.
You know, Buntline, when I first came here, there was
nothing, with a capital 'no.' I lived here alone for years
without laying eyes on another human face. Then that
robot probe landed from Diversicorp. Damn thing landed

20 meters from me. Just about scared me out of my pants
I kept expecting a bunch of short aliens to come out of
it. The only thing that came out of it was this big arm—
scooping up dirt, scooping up dirt. Craziest thing I ever
saw. I knew right away what it meant—civilization. The
ecological rapists would be there any minute. I walked
over and studied the probe a few minutes. I told myself I
had to do something. I got a shovel—"

"I thought all you had was a Bowie knife, Uncle."

"Shut up, Eldridge. I got my shovel and dumped some
dirt into that robot scoop—worst looking dirt I could find.
That, Bentspine, was my mistake."

"Why?"

"Isn't it obvious?"

"No."

"The stuff was high-grade pyraclore ore. The robot
analyzed it and sent off its message. By the time I realized
what I'd done, it was too late. People—hordes of people—
were coming."

"Five thousand people is hardly a horde, Uncle."

"It's a horde when you're all alone. I had no choice but
to do what I did."

"What did you do?"

Jacobson gestured about at the lobby again. "Built this
place."

Benson saw an opportunity to dig behind the pose. "And
you get your entire livelihood from this hotel?"

Abruptly, Jacobson dropped the pose, his eyes narrowing. He looked intently at Benson. "So what, Benson?"

"If Morris's plan for Paria had been adopted and all
human activity on the planet had stopped, you would have
been out a lot of money."

Jacobson snorted. "What are you suggesting?"

"Nothing. I'm just stating a fact. It is a fact, isn't it?"

Jacobson's face began to redden even more behind the

eard. "I don't think I like you as much as I used to, Benson. Why don't you get the hell out of my sight?"

Benson began to say something. Before he could, Jacobson abruptly turned away and started for the stairs, walking tick thumping with every other step. He called back over his shoulder to Eldridge without looking around. "And get them cockroaches out of the kitchen, you worthless monkey's uncle."

Eldridge, embarrassed, looked at Benson and shrugged. "My uncle has strong opinions. Sorry about that, Mr. Benson. Sometimes he doesn't realize how it looks when he says the things he says."

"What are you trying to tell me, Eldridge?"

"That I understand why you asked my uncle that question about the money and that he had nothing to do with Morris's mindwiping."

"Are you sure of that, Eldridge?"

Eldridge remained silent, biting his lip.

CHAPTER 12

Benson walked through the static field. The warm air outside hit his face. As he walked, he thought he could feel his nose begin to dry up. The cold had continued to bother him. Nothing he took for it seemed to help.

He had eaten lunch at the hotel bar and decided to talk to Cowdin. Now that Benson knew more about the conditions on Paria, the engineer might be able to help. He gazed around at the flat landscape. He remembered the tape of Schwab senselessly running out here, scrambling up the side of one of the mounds. What people did when they were frightened continually amazed Benson. Given a choice, innocent people invariably chose the most incriminating course of action. They picked up the murder weapon at the scene of the crime or they fled. They said the one wrong thing, usually to the police. Each time they made a decision in their panicked state, they made the situation worse for themselves and added work for Benson.

He shrugged off the thought, recognizing it as a symptom of the cold. Benson always began to feel overburdened when he had a cold. Ahead, he finally saw what he was looking for, a small, plastone building halfway between the edge of the concession and the beginning of the Parian mounds. Cowdin had his working office in the building. As general operations manager of the Diversicorp interests on Paria—in spite of Benson's personal reaction to the man—Cowdin might actually be able to provide some useful information.

Benson changed course toward the building, wondering why Cowdin had constructed his office beyond the limits of the concession. Diversicorp supplied him with one that must be the equal of the governor's in the hotel. It took several seconds to realize the answer. If the mining company's officers were in the hotel, supervision of any of the barter with the natives would be easily controlled. With facilities nearer the mounds, the company could conduct its business without constant interference from Finnley. At the same time, the Parians themselves would not have to enter the human colony. If what Schwab had said about the creature's smell was at all accurate, that might be sufficient reason in itself. It would also expedite the barter, conducting all the trade on the Parians' home ground.

Benson reached the building and pressed the callplate next to the door. The small screen above the plate lit immediately. Cowdin's rugged face appeared in it. He recognized Benson at once and smiled.

"Ah, Mr. Benson. What can I do for you?"

"I'd like to talk to you about Governor Morris, if it's not too much trouble."

"No trouble at all. I'll be right up."

Cowdin's face disappeared from the screen. Benson could make nothing of the man's tone of voice. He would have to wait until they talked face to face to get any definite impression. Seeing Cowdin in his own surroundings, rather than the impersonal environment of a shuttleport or a starship, might help resolve the puzzle behind the man.

The door next to the callplate slid back. Cowdin smiled and invited Benson into his "humble abode." They passed several rooms, living quarters, eating area and arrived finally at an office.

The office looked more like that of a scholar than that of someone responsible for the Diversicorp mining operations. Papers and manuals were stacked meticulously on tables around the room. A large desk stood in back of Cowdin, also stacked with papers. On the desk, pens, pencils, a voicewriter microphone and other materials were arranged in neat succession across the surface. The room indicated a meticulous man, one careful with details and, probably, people.

Looking closely at Cowdin for the first time, Benson guessed his age to be about 40. In the shuttleport on Earth and on the starship, Benson had had little desire to think about Cowdin. Since finding out that Cowdin was indeed what he purported to be, along with the accident aboard the *Liberty*, Benson took a renewed interest in the man. Cowdin had a weathered look about him, as though he had spent many years working outdoors and had arrived where he was now by that work. His eyes returned Benson's gaze crisply and directly.

Cowdin, his voice as rough naturally as Benson's was with the cold, asked now he could help. "My secretary in the hotel phoned me that you were coming. Anything I can do to help—as I said—I'll be happy to do. We'd hate to lose Mr. Schwab. I understand he was a very efficient employee."

"Did you know Schwab personally, Mr. Cowdin?"

"No. But of course, after he was picked up, rumors got back to me from astronauts and through the company grapevine. The general consensus of opinion seemed to be shock. Schwab was well liked by his co-workers. They found it difficult to believe that he would do such a thing."

"At the time, Mr. Schwab was unaware of any telepathic ability. I doubt he would have even thought himself capable of it."

"Ah, I see. That was the one point they all kept insisting on. How could he do it without the ability, rather like trying to shoot someone with a toy gun? But you say it has been established that Mr. Schwab is telepathic."

Benson nodded.

"I thought so. When the question arose here, I checked Schwab's personnel file. I thought I could see indications of some latent ability in it."

"Mr. Cowdin, you don't have any idea why Schwab was originally called to the surface of Paria, do you?"

"Doesn't he know?"

Benson noticed that Cowdin's face showed a properly incredulous expression. He knew too little to speculate whether it meant anything.

"No. Schwab says he was called here and no reason was given. The way he put it was 'if the brass wanted him, the brass could have him.' They were paying for it and the room was supposed to be air-conditioned."

Cowdin smiled. Being one of the "brass," the thought no doubt amused him. It would be better to be on Cowdin's good side, especially after virtually snubbing him during the trip from Earth.

Cowdin became pensive. "I really don't have the slightest idea why Mr. Schwab would have been called down here. The various divisions within Diversicorp, although coordinated to the overall interests of the company and managed according to similar policies, are autonomous when it comes to personnel. I occasionally forget there are divisions other than this mining operation. I'm sorry Gordon Olmstead isn't on Paria just now. He's the transportation division's liaison man. He might know more about it."

Benson remained silent, hoping his expectation of something more would draw Cowdin out.

Cowdin thought a moment, then continued. "I could try to find out if there is any information available on the matter at Gordon's office. Gordon runs a pretty tight ship over there. In spite of the fact that I've been looking in on his office during his absence, he would probably be the only one who would know."

Benson watched Cowdin turn and look out the window, then wave an arm to direct Benson's attention to the scene. "Have you been on Paria before, Mr. Benson?"

"No."

"Most people would say that was fortunate, except, perhaps, Max Jacobson. Do you know Max?"

"I talked with him briefly. He has strong opinions on Paria."

"Max hates any kind of development. He would be just as happy to see this concession wither away to nothing. In many ways, I can understand his feelings. I rather like this place, too. I can imagine that a man like yourself, a man with several academic degrees to his credit and the interest an educated man must take in the world about him, can appreciate that there are things to learn anywhere one goes." Cowdin nodded toward the monotonous landscape outside the window. It spread from horizon to horizon, broken only by the Parian mounds. To Benson's eyes, it looked utterly devoid of interest. "Even in a place like this," concluded Cowdin.

Benson nodded. "Yes, I suppose even a desolate spot like this can teach something, though it's difficult for the uninitiated to see what." Benson looked at the landscape, at a loss for anything more insightful to add to Cowdin's remarks but wanting to let Cowdin show more of himself than he had until then.

Cowdin, noticing Benson's disposition to stay and listen, continued. "Take the Parians themselves, for example. Our new governor, Mr. Finnley—have you talked to him yet, by the way?"

"I wasn't aware he had arrived."

"Just this morning. I was part of the official welcoming party. He seemed to be full of opinions about our Parians, though I doubt that he has ever actually seen one. I offered to introduce him. He declined. He considers them idiotic creatures. He thinks it useless for them to tunnel under half a continent." Cowdin's face momentarily lit up. "That's how far the networks currently extend, Mr. Benson—half a continent! It's utterly marvelous!" Cowdin's face returned to impassivity. "But not to Governor Finnley. He is almost a caricature of the ethnocentric man. I tried to point out to him that the Parians, no doubt, think it pointless for us to pack dirt in long silver tubes and shoot it up in the air as we do. From their point of view, it is an equally foolish activity. Philosophically, they consider dirt as something to be gotten out of the way in order to reveal a tunnel. That anyone would actually *want* the dirt seems to them the height of folly."

"It sounds to me very much like you're personifying them a little yourself."

Cowdin shrugged. "Possibly, a little. They would not actually conceptualize the problem the way I have stated it. They would simply act on it, remove the dirt to reveal the tunnel, then forget the dirt. Still, it amounts to the same thing, doesn't it, Mr. Benson?"

"I suppose so."

"In any case, I tried to explain this to Governor Finnley. In his opinion it is perfectly obvious that the ore that produces tantalum and niobium and is in turn used in everything from starship drives to apartment house reactors is not a useless product, nor is the activity of getting it a useless activity." Cowdin glanced at Benson. "Are you at all interested in this, Mr. Benson? At times, it borders on a personal obsession with me."

"You don't seem too impressed with your new governor," said Benson, avoiding the question and hoping to draw Cowdin out.

"Frankly, Mr. Benson, he is a fool. I suspect he is a bit paranoid as well. I noticed intimations in our conversation of this morning that indicate he believes the entire federation hierarchy is out to get him personally, to retard his career and leave him forever in the remote provinces. A man like that might well have motives for getting rid of people he suspects stand in the way of his advancement, Mr. Benson. Governor Morris, on the other hand, was no fool. A brilliant man, an inquisitive mind, thoroughly my equal in understanding the situation we have here on Paria."

"But Finnley wasn't on Paria when Morris was mind-wiped—that is, if you're implying he had something to do with it."

"I'm not implying anything. I am simply stating what I have observed. Finnley is an unstable personality. He has been relegated to this planet, which he considers a back-water world, because of his own incompetence. He was not here *officially* at the time of Morris's mindwiping, but he was here, in transit to Earth for reassignment. I brought that very matter up with him today. He denied it of course. Yet the federation guest suite at Jacobson's hotel bears his name for the dates involved. He finally admitted it and claimed to have forgotten it completely. I am not saying Governor Finnley was in any way involved, but I do find the coincidence of dates interesting. I just want this man Schwab to have as fair a chance as possible and to do that, you have to know all the facts, don't you, Mr. Benson? That Finnley was here at the time of Morris's mindwiping is a fact, easily verifiable."

"I appreciate your telling me, Mr. Cowdin."

Cowdin returned his attention to the window and the landscape outside. "Yes, Mr. Benson, I have tried to explain the Parian's view of our activities to many people, Finnley included. I become, I'm afraid, quite disgusted with his type of stupidity. I told him to explain his own views to the Parians, and while he was at it, he could let them explain why they tunnel. For what may appear absurd to our eyes, both in the general and the existential sense of the word, is the very essence of Parian life. Have you ever read any xenobiology or anthrozoology, Mr. Benson?"

"Only in college," answered Benson, disquieted by the atmosphere of Cowdin's conversation, though with no idea why. The content seemed innocent enough. Benson had trained himself early to be sensitive to atmosphere. The most delicate negotiations for Benson's clients had often been successful more through his attention to atmosphere than to the content of the transaction. Still, he found it difficult to pinpoint the exact quality in Cowdin's atmosphere that unsettled him.

"It is a fascinating field, Mr. Benson, especially for one who has traveled to many worlds. The habits of creatures within the human range of culture and intelligence and most especially the reasons they give for doing what they do—like our Parians out there—are endlessly interesting to me. Studying such things, one is studying more the philosophy than the mere biology of a species. In the universe, all things are possible. Anything—literally anything—can exist. I have heard the view maintained that when anything is possible, everything is boring. I take that to mean that the unique quality is lost, the salient, distinguishing feature is lost from view in the general wash of sameness."

Cowdin hesitated a moment and glanced at Benson. "I do not share that view, Mr. Benson. When anything is possible, the particular way in which something has worked itself out is utterly fascinating. Take ourselves, for example. We are a product of evolution on an Earth-type planet. That evolution could have taken courses much different from those it did take. We could be creatures with four arms like the Trodes of Wolff-275-6. It would make very little difference from a survival viewpoint. It might even have been an advantage for our biological ancestors, the ability to run at the high speeds permitted by four legs, yet at the same time throw rocks at our pursuers with the remaining two arms." Cowdin smiled slightly, anticipating his next comment. "Even in our own high state of civilization and culture, a common complaint is not having more than two hands. What is interesting is the way in fact nature has developed, the reality of the situation. Amid the plethora of possibilities, one has emerged and we are that one."

"You find the Parians fascinating as well?"

Cowdin looked out the window toward the mounds. "The studies on the Parians are, unfortunately, inadequate. I have tried from time to time to fill in some of the holes in the picture with my own efforts at observation and explanation. I have published several articles on the matter—" Cowdin looked at Benson, smiling weakly again "—all of course in obscure journals. None of the mass media outlets would handle the material." He returned his attention to the mounds. "Poor Morris helped me on many occasions. He was a brilliant man, as I have said. And his understanding was not limited to the Parians. He understood men as well. He understood men considerably better than our current fool of a governor."

"They always say that the qualities of the observer are reflected in his observations," said Benson, quoting a dimly remembered platitude from some mandatory undergraduate science class.

"Quite true, Mr. Benson. Morris knew Parians because he knew men. There is something of men in the Parians. Finnley will never see that. He thinks them rats and nothing more. Finnley understands neither men nor Parians. He does not understand that we and the Parians both exist at this instant in space-time, and that fact alone gives us more in common than we have as differences. Do you see their mounds out there, Mr. Benson? Interesting, aren't they?"

They just looked like mounds to Benson. He said nothing.

"Do you have any idea what they are for?"

"Light and air in their tunnels, I imagine."

"That and more. To our eyes, they appear to be arranged in a random pattern. Actually, the pattern is rigidly apparent to the Parians. Each mound is placed in the pattern that is dictated by certain principles they have developed over the eons, a system that would take me hours to explain. I am currently working on an article that will explain them, both the principles behind the pattern itself and the religious-philosophical-sociological significance of the pattern to the Parians. I believe it to be a product of their dream life. Men try to build from conscious inspiration—at least we usually do. But the Parians build according to the promptings of their dreams as it relates to their concept of a well-ordered universe. The fact that they dream at all is enough of a revelation. It is amazing to me. But the fact that they aspire—that, Mr. Benson, is incredible. They work constantly. They plan constantly. In their simple way, they plan thoroughly. To them, we are only a means to obtain better tools to allow them to create the network of their world to fit their dreams.

"Men, too, often dream and plan. But the plans of men are often at cross-purposes. They have none of the concerted community of effort so visible in the Parians. The Parians conceive of society as the basic unit of identity. They tolerate no individualism that would destroy the harmony of that society. What do you make of that, Mr. Benson?"

"I suppose it's our nature to be as we are and theirs to be as they are. I wonder if I could make one request of you, Mr. Cowdin?"

"Of course. Anything I can do to help. I mean that sincerely."

"Do you happen to know a woman—probably about 25—named Regina Quinton? No one else seems to know her, but I have reason to believe she's on Paria."

Cowdin's expression remained unchanged, yet Benson thought he could almost feel Cowdin's rapture with his discourse fade. The atmosphere, Benson noted, had changed slightly.

Cowdin shook his head. "No, I don't believe I know anyone by that name. Do you have any other information on her? Does she work for us?"

"I don't know."

"I'll check," said Cowdin. He walked to the phone and punched out a two-digit number. A young woman's face came on the screen, alert and ready to respond to questions.

"Ms. Wells, would you check our personnel files and see whether we have someone named Regina—" Cowdin glanced at Benson, eyebrows raised.

"Quinton."

"Regina Quinton. See if we have anyone by that name working for us, will you please?"

"Yes, sir," Ms. Wells responded and left the screen for several minutes. Benson and Cowdin waited in silence until she returned. She came on the screen shaking her head. "We have no one whose name even begins with Q working for us on Paria, sir."

"Thank you." Cowdin touched off the phone. "I guess I can't be of any help there either, Mr. Benson. I will check at Mr. Olmstead's office and see what I can find out for you. But, as I said, I don't expect much. This is a small place. I'm sure I would have heard the name if such a person were working for any of our divisions here."

Benson could see the conversation was at an end. He shook hands with Cowdin again. "Thank you for your help, Mr. Cowdin. And for your insights into Parian behavior."

"Anytime. If I find anything concerning this Quinton woman, I'll contact you at the hotel."

"Fine, thank you. I may need your help again. May I call on you?"

"Of course. I'm here most of the time."

Benson, wondering about the faint uneasiness he felt in Cowdin's presence, left.

CHAPTER 13

During the walk back to the concession, Benson noticed the beneficial effects of the warm air on his cold. His nose felt as though it were at last drying up and his mind was clearer. At the same time, he found it difficult to shake off the odd sensation he had felt during the conversation with Cowdin. Nothing in the content of the conversation justified the sensation. He kept returning to one point: atmosphere.

He passed through the static field at the edge of the concession. During his few days on Paria, his picture of the situation had clarified substantially. Morris, the up-and-coming, well-thought-of governor of the planet had enemies. Though Cowdin had gone out of his way to praise Morris as a man of substantial ability, he had also made it clear that their views of official policy on exploitation of the planet were diametrically opposed. Morris wanted the Parians off-limits as subjects for exploitation. Cowdin, in charge of Diversicorp's activities, wanted the exploitation to continue. In fact, Cowdin felt the exploitation helped the Parians carry out their own designs. Benson reminded himself to find out how close Morris was to realizing his plan when he was mindwiped.

In addition, Max Jacobson was at cross-purposes with Governor Morris, or at least thought he was. On the one hand, Max seemed the rugged frontiersman disgusted with the coming of progress and civilization. If this represented his true feelings—something Benson doubted—Max as the third political force on the planet could want a return to the good old days. He could have thought of Morris as the prime exponent of the progress he hated and thought that by removing him he could retard, prevent or even roll back progress.

But Max's arch-reactionary manner struck Benson as only a pose. When Max, angered, turned and walked away from Benson, something of his true position seemed to show. Prior to the arrival of the human colony on Paria, Max had lived the romantic life of the interstellar prospector, searching out his fortune alone on remote worlds. In fact, that life was lonely and unprofitable for the people living it. Max had been no exception. The coming of the colony to Paria meant one thing to Max—it was a chance to make the fortune that had escaped him all his life. In addition, Max would certainly know about Morris's plan to leave Paria and the Parians to themselves and allow them to develop intellectually and culturally on their own. If, abruptly, the human colony pulled up stakes and left, they would take any chance Max had of making a fortune with them.

And Finnley too, the man Benson was about to see, had reasons to wish Morris out of the way. Assuming Cowdin's impressions of Finnley corresponded to something like reality, Finnley could have believed either that Morris was somehow blocking his chances for advancement, or, by disappearing, would allow it. Benson would have to see Finnley to obtain a better reading.

At the hotel, Benson nodded courteously to Eldridge Jacobson—who, instead of trying to remain immobile as long as possible behind the check-in desk, was now making a dustcloud near the door with a broom—and went upstairs to his room. He checked it thoroughly to make sure nothing had been tampered with and left again, starting down the corridor to Finnley's—formerly Morris's—office. He passed the door he remembered from Schwab's kineticorder tape, now closed, and turned in at the door to the office proper. A middle-aged woman sat behind a desk with several neatly stacked piles of computer printout before her.

Benson approached her. "My name is Benson. I'd like to see Governor Finnley, if that's possible."

The woman barely glanced up from the papers. "Concerning what, may I ask?"

"It's official business."

"Official business can cover a multitude of sins. Please be more specific. The governor is a busy man. As you no doubt know, he only arrived this morning. He has a lot of familiarization to do before he can concern himself with trivial matters."

"Do you consider Governor Morris's mindwiping trivial?"

The woman's finger hesitated, about to turn a page on a printout. She looked up. "In what way are you connected with that incident?"

"I represent Ernest Schwab."

The woman's face soured, her disgust evident. "I'm sorry, the governor does not have time for the likes of you. As I said, he is a busy man."

"Why don't we let him decide that?"

"Because I am deciding it."

"Do you have the authority to decide whom the governor will and will not see?"

She fixed Benson with an even, angry stare. "Mr. Benson, I have always had the authority to say who is allowed to see the governor. Before the vicious act that obliterated one of the finest men I have ever known occurred, I had the sole authority for who saw the governor. I managed Jeremy's—I mean Governor Morris's—time and never received a complaint. I expect to continue that function. I do not intend to have anything to do with freeing the vicious creature who did that thing to Governor Morris. Governor Morris was like a son to me." She hesitated.

"More than a son. I do not intend to let you do anything to besmirch his memory."

"I don't intend to besmirch anything. All I want to find out is the truth."

"Mr. Benson, *I* know the truth. That telepath of yours destroyed one of the finest men who ever lived. That destruction was utter and final. The sooner the same end comes to the man who did it, the sooner we will have justice and the truth."

"You can't deny me an interview with Governor Finnley."

"I can and will."

From across the room, Benson heard someone clear his throat. He looked away from the secretary. The door to the inner office stood open, a man in the doorway.

"Did you wish to see me about something, Mr.—"

"Benson. Yes, Governor, I do want to see you. It's about your predecessor's mindwiping."

Governor Finnley frowned slightly, then glanced at the secretary. "Miss Childs, why didn't you inform me Mr. Benson was here?"

"Mr. Benson represents Ernest Schwab, the telepath who . . . who. . . ." Her voice faltered.

"Yes, yes. Well, in the future, Miss Childs, let me decide whom I will see and whom I won't. Do you understand that?"

"Yes, sir, but—"

"No buts. I will decide what is important and what is trivial." Finnley looked at Benson. "Will you step this way, Mr. Benson. We can talk in my office."

Benson followed Finnley into the office. Almost before the door had completely closed, Finnley's look of composure had vanished, replaced by anger. "I have to apologize for that woman, Mr. Benson. It is hard enough for me to take up my duties on this godforsaken rat-hole planet. On top of it, I have to compete with the ghost of this Morris person. She worshipped Morris. They tell me any reference to Morris caused her to break down and sob for a week after the event. She is only now beginning to become coherent again." Finnley returned to the other side of his desk, motioned for Benson to sit down and plopped into his own chair. "You wanted to talk to me about this mindwiper of yours."

"I wanted to talk to you about Ernest Schwab."

"Same thing. I had a very interesting conversation on that very subject with an extremely sympathetic gentleman aboard the starship that brought me here, very interesting indeed," said Finnley and hesitated a moment to emphasize his next remark, "under the circumstances."

Benson understood neither the emphasis nor the remark. "What circumstances?"

Finnley grunted. "I'm sure you're as conversant with them as I am—probably more so. What is it you wanted to talk to me about?"

Whatever Finnley meant by his "circumstances," Benson could see the governor held him partially responsible. Though Benson was glad enough that Finnley had found a sympathetic ear aboard the starship, for his own part, he preferred to stay close to the business at hand, rather than antagonize Finnley by discussing vague and probably irrelevant circumstances. "Have you had an opportunity to go over any of Morris's papers?"

"I have been doing nothing else since I was posted here. On Earth, they gave me a document file disk containing all his papers, both personal and official. By the way, Mr. Benson, you look ill. Are you? It's impossible to tell who's ill and who isn't in the blasted light on this blasted world."

"I'm just getting over a cold. The air here seems to be helping it. Was there anything in Morris's papers that—"

"I don't mind telling you, Mr. Benson, I don't like these fellows."

"Which fellows?"

"Telepaths—especially criminal telepaths."

"I don't think criminals are too popular anywhere."

"But telepathic criminals—there's something about them that makes me slightly—" Finnley's face turned momentarily sour "—uncomfortable, if you know what I mean."

"The unpredictability."

"Exactly. Somehow they don't seem quite human. Your man, for example, has done something we all would have thought a human being incapable of."

"I'm not so sure he's done it."

"What about afterward—he certainly did that."

Benson, assuming Finnley meant Schwab's attempt to flee from the security guards after the mindwiping, nodded. "It's quite common under the circumstances."

"Common! To my knowledge, it's never happened!"

"I'm afraid your knowledge may be somewhat limited. Even innocent men often feel threatened in such circumstances. Desperation causes men to do strange things."

Finnley's face turned grim. "But they seldom get away with it. As to my legal knowledge, Mr. Benson, I do not want you to make any mistake about that. During my own youth, I, too, wanted to be a lawyer. I did not, however, have an opportunity to finish law school. Unlike my predecessor, who was given everything on a silver platter, I have had to work for everything I got. I had to work then. It interfered with my studies."

"You flunked out."

"On the contrary, I would have received the highest marks in the class if it had not been for several people who were out to get me. Oh, I know how that sounds. Nevertheless, it is true. People have been out to get me from the beginning of my career. And now, here I am in this rat hole. They've got me at last. Oh, this kind of place was all right for people like Jeremy Morris." Finnley spit out the name. "A man on the way up can afford to be stuck in a place like this for a few years. It might even be considered a kind of tribute to Morris's ability, a governor at 30. But for me—for a man who has already served his time on half the insignificant planets in the federation—it is almost the end of the line. I am 53 years old, Mr. Benson. I have only one more chance for a decent appointment. The fact that they have given me this pockmarked world in the middle of nowhere to govern shows someone lacks the proper confidence in my abilities. They are wrong, of course, completely, utterly and hopelessly wrong, but—" Finnley shrugged "—it is the burden I must bear. If I handle matters well here—and, Mr. Benson, I assure you I intend to do just that—my next appointment will be closer to Earth. I do not intend to aid, in any way, shape or form, kill-crazed telepaths."

"I'm not asking you to."

"It certainly sounded very close to that."

"In the first place, I assure you, I have talked with Mr. Schwab and he is in all other respects perfectly normal."

"Normal? A mindwiper! Ha!"

"Normal or not, he does have the same rights as anyone else. And those rights do have to be protected. You can understand that, I'm sure."

"Certainly. I suppose Jack the Ripper's rights would have to be upheld no matter what you thought of Jack the Ripper personally."

"Exactly."

"You know, Mr. Benson, sometimes I wonder about a system that allows such things. Are you at all familiar with the ancient Earth cultures?"

"Some of them."

"The ancient Greeks?"

"Yes."

"An admirable people. They developed almost every political system we have seen active in the history of mankind. Sometimes I think we would do well to emulate them."

"Which system in particular did you have in mind?"

"Sparta—oh, not the military aristocracy aspect of Spartan life. That I would find abhorent on general principles. It was more the fitness-to-live aspect of their culture that I refer to. Do you know the Spartans examined each baby born to the population? If it appeared to be unfit, they did away with it, smashed its little head against a rock or some such thing. At times, I think we should reinstitute that practice."

"For telepaths only, of course."

Finnley nodded. "Precisely." He smiled. "Just an idea, of course. I would probably look somewhat inhuman if I passed such a suggestion up the chain of command, though it's still worth thinking about."

"Governor Finnley, let me get one thing clear before we start doing away with all telepaths. It hasn't yet been established that Mr. Schwab did anything criminal with any ability he may or may not have."

"Yes, yes. I appreciate that. And at this late date in our civilization, I do not suppose my suggestion would be considered practical. I certainly would not want to be responsible for sending a perfectly innocent man—assuming, for the moment, that your man is innocent—"

"I believe him to be so."

"Of course you do, Benson. What else could you believe in your position?" Finnley waved aside this irrelevancy. "But what you believe is, as you lawyers say, immaterial. Yet let's pursue this thought of mine a few steps further, if that's all right with you."

Benson glanced at his watch. "You're sure you have the time for it, Governor Finnley?"

Finnley pooh-poohed the idea. "There is always time for stimulating discussion, Benson. We get so little of it out here on these frontier worlds. The same faces day in and day out. Nothing to break the monotony but an occasional sunstroke. And time, that's about all we do have out here."

"I see you've made a quick adjustment to your new post."

"One has to be flexible. Let us suppose, Benson, that we have some way of detecting future criminality in infants, children who would grow up and become psychopathic killers. The system is utterly foolproof, we shall say. Every child tagged as a future psychopath will become just that. No exceptions. He will grow up to murder, rape and burgle."

"Burglarize."

Finnley ignored the correction. "As I said, the system is perfect by definition. Children cleared by it will never murder, rape or . . . burglarize. In that case, would you approve or disapprove of doing away with those found to be defective?"

"Doing away with them in what sense?"

"Slitting their spindly throats or anything you like. They are 100 percent certifiable psychopaths, remember."

"That particular method of getting rid of them sounds a little inhuman."

"Does the method matter? Pick your own method."

"I would probably accept a rehabilitation mindwipe."

"And if that proved unsuccessful?"

"Fortunately, we aren't faced with that problem."

"But if we were, how would you vote? Life? Or death?"

"Governor Finnley, I find this conversation a bit gruesome. Do you think we could—"

"Queasy stomach, eh?"

"Not particularly. I would just prefer to stick to the point."

"I'll tell you what I find a bit gruesome, Benson." Governor Finnley leaned forward, one elbow on the desk, pointing at Benson. "I find it gruesome that telepaths—criminal telepaths—are free at this very moment in our society. I find it gruesome that such a criminal telepath would feel he could mindwipe the governor of this very colony and get away with it. I find that whole idea gruesome! And I am prepared to take measures to insure there is no repeat performance. Is that understood?"

"Governor, all I want to do is look into Mr. Schwab's case, I do not have any plans to loose him on this colony."

"But what are his plans, Benson?"

"To clear himself. I wanted to check with you to see if the investigation on the incident had gone any further."

"Further! What do you mean? The man was arrested and put in jail. What more do they want? If that isn't enough, the man fled. That clearly shows—"

"He was scared."

"That isn't the way I hear it. I hear he was brazen and self-assured."

"I think you're hearing wrong. In any case, there is still the question of Schwab's guilt to be considered."

Agitated beyond any ability to control it, Finnley stood up, attempting to tower over Benson. "Guilt! For heaven's sake, man, they walked right in after that maniac had turned poor Morris into a husk! How could he be less guilty?"

"That's what I'm trying to establish."

"And you will not succeed."

"I'll have to decide that for myself. Did Morris leave any papers or documents behind?"

"Benson," said Finnley, sitting down. "I have been over all of this with a colleague of yours, a man named Mc-Masters. He called here several hours ago. He asked the same kind of questions you are asking. I will give you the same answers I gave him. I have the collection of all Governor Morris's papers. I plan to pass them along to the proper authorities. They are unavailable—as you should know government papers would be—to anyone without the proper clearances."

"I could have them subpoenaed."

"Then do so. I refuse to release federation documents to just anyone who happens to walk into my office. That is what I told Mr. McMasters. That is what I tell you. There are no exceptions to the rule." Finnley smiled. "I do not wish to seem uncooperative, but I do have my duty. Benson, I assure you, I have read all of Morris's papers, both government and private. There is nothing in them that can make the slightest bit of difference to this telepath's case."

Benson tried to look unconvinced.

"For either side, Benson—yours or McMasters."

"I may have them subpoenaed anyway." Benson stood up, preparing to leave. "By the way, you don't happen to know someone named Regina Quinton, do you?"

"Quinton? Quinton?" Finnley thought. "The name doesn't ring a bell."

"Thank you, Governor. You don't mind if I continue looking around your little colony?"

"Not at all. I will, as far as my official duties will allow me, help you in any way I can."

Benson had a suspicion Finnley's official duties would not allow him to be excessively helpful. "Thank you, again, Governor."

Benson walked to the door and out. In the outer office, tracked by the scowling glare of Miss Childs, he approached the door to the corridor. Just as he reached it, Finnley's voice, made tinny by the small loudspeaker, burst into the room on the intercom.

"Miss Childs, will you please bring me everything you can find on someone named Regina Quinton? She is supposed to be a resident of this godforsaken rat hole."

Benson walked the short distance down the corridor to his room. His interview with Finnley had convinced him of one thing. The man had nothing to do with mindwiping Morris. The sincerity of his hatred for his new post was beyond question. Given a choice, Finnley would have kept Morris active in order to keep the post filled and unavailable to him.

Benson entered his room, again scanning it to make sure nothing had been searched. He paced the room a few minutes, thinking. Either Jacobson or Cowdin could have been responsible—but how? That was the question. Once he knew how, he would know who.

On one pass of the window, Benson happened to glance out. Movement across the street caught his attention. He stopped and peered into the street.

A man.

The shadows of late afternoon made it impossible for Benson to see who he was, but his instinctive reaction, bred over years of criminal investigation, told him that he was going to meet the stranger face-to-face before long.

How could he get a closer look now? His eyes darted about the room and noticed the phone with its built-in camera lens. He walked over to it, picked it up and carried it back to the window. He turned it so that the camera pointed outside.

Then he waited.

In a minute or so, the man moved, his face coming into the dull sunlight.

Benson positioned the phone on the window ledge, standing to one side yet able to see the small monitor screen. After he touched it on, color static played across its surface. The faint tone of an open line reached his ears.

The screen filled with the doorway and the man.

. . . *Schwab!*

REGINA

The man Schwab has returned. I do not like the man Schwab. Mr. Cowdin has told me about him. The man Schwab has been acting bad again like the other time. He was made to act good but now he acts bad again. He is like so many people. I rest my cheek against the organdy pillow—my favorite. I think. One day, we will be able to make more people nice than just one. Mr. Cowdin has assured me of that. He has told me many times that we will be able, one day, to make hundreds, thousands— possibly millions—of people act good. The idea gives me a warm and comfortable feeling.

I do not like thinking how mean people are. It upsets me. I move my legs into a more comfortable position and adjust my long, loose shift to cover my knees. If only people were nicer. If only they treated each other better. But they do not. I dislike living here but I dislike living with people the way they are now. They have been mean to me all of my life. When I was a girl, they were mean to me because I was a telepath. I could not help being a telepath any more than they could help being non-telepaths. Still, they were mean to me. They made me live outside the city. There were no other children to play with. Even though I could not help being what I am, people shunned and avoided me. It is unpleasant to remember.

Even now, when I can control what they hear in their minds, they are mean to me. My appearance disturbs them. But I must eat—everyone must eat. It is one of my few pleasures. Only Mr. Cowdin is nice to me, sometimes. But those rat creatures are awful. They are dirty and stupid and I feel shivers when I see them. They smell bad.

I lean back and contemplate the giant stuffed panda from Earth. It is nice. They will all be nice. Mr. Cowdin and I will make them all be nice. They will be at one with themselves and I will be accepted by them. It is what Mr. Cowdin has promised.

CHAPTER 14

Schwab slapped depilatory on his face and wiped away his beard. He stared at himself in the mirror. He was beginning to look somewhat more like a respectable citizen and less like an escaped criminal. Two days of hiding in warehouses on Paria had left him looking scruffy. The shower and wipe had helped.

Out of the corner of his eye, he could see Benson watching him from the main part of the hotel room. Benson looked annoyed. Since Schwab had made his way up the back stairs in the hotel to Benson's room, Benson had looked annoyed, or worse. Schwab finished wiping his face and went into the room.

"Why, Schwab," said Benson, the annoyance also clear in his voice, "did you do it?"

Schwab's face became plaintive. "I had to, Mr. Benson. I had to contribute something to my own defense. Can't you see that?"

"No, I can't. All you've done is make things worse for yourself. It has the same effect as when you fled after the mindwipe. It makes you look that much more guilty. Utterly irresponsible!"

Schwab continued to plead. "I know all that, Mr. Benson, but I couldn't just sit in that cell and do nothing."

Benson shook his head, disgust clear on his face. "I ought to turn you over to the authorities immediately."

"Mr. Benson, I had to do it, especially when I remembered the footprints. I couldn't trust that information to a normal phone system. Phones—even subspace phones—

153

are too susceptible to a tap. I don't know who's involved here on Paria. It could be anyone. They could be in a position to pick up any message I sent or keep it from getting to you."

Benson's annoyance seemed to pass. Evidently, he thought the explanation had some merit. "Okay, tell me about the footprint."

Schwab started to tell Benson about his last moments in the tunnels. The phone glowed, interrupting. Benson waved Schwab into one corner of the room out of view of the phone camera and answered it. Schwab recognized the voice on the other end as that of McMasters, the Federation Prosecutor.

"Benson, I've been trying to get hold of you for the past five days. They said you couldn't be contacted while your ship was in hyperspace. And you've been out of your room everytime I called."

"You could have left a message."

"Yes, yes, yes. I could have. But I didn't. I thought you might want to hear this straight from me. That raging lunatic telepath of yours has escaped. He threatened to mindwipe everyone from here to Alpha Centauri."

Schwab could see Benson's face. It remained unchanged at the revelation. "I heard. Looks to me like the authorities on Earth were asleep at the switch."

"Asleep at the switch! What the hell would you have done? The man mindwiped one person already. We had no idea what the extent of his power was. We had to let him go. I'll be frank with you, Benson. When I called your office and found out where you had gone on this so-called health holiday of yours, I knew you were as healthy as I am."

"I do have a cold. I can get it certified if you like. The warm air here seems to be helping it."

"A certification will not be necessary, nor a note from your mother. But I warn you, if this whole thing is just some kind of delay to give that man of yours a chance to escape, you are not going to be an attorney for very much longer. You may even need one yourself."

"I didn't have anything to do with the escape, Mc-Masters. You can have my word on that. I just learned about it today. If you want to bring some kind of charges against me, okay. That's your privilege. But make sure you get all your facts straight before you start something like that. I am prepared to take my own legal action if you spread any rumors to that effect."

"I hope you're telling me the truth, Benson. Whether you are or aren't, this incident has just about given me the case."

"You're sure about that?"

"So you do know something about it!"

"Did I say that?"

"No, but your face—"

"My face what?"

"Nothing. That's just the point. Your face didn't do anything. And you had to strain to keep it from doing anything. Don't play poker, Benson. You're bad at it. Your face is a dead giveaway."

"McMasters, I've told you everything I can. I didn't know anything about the escape until after the fact. Anything else I know comes under the attorney-client privilege. That's it. Now, if you don't have anything else to say—"

Schwab heard the quality of McMasters's voice change. Since the escape, McMasters had probably had very little sleep, less than Schwab. His voice sounded tired and distracted.

"I'll tell you something, Benson, though I really shouldn't, all things considered."

"What?"

"I really admire him in some ways."

"Who?"

"Schwab. That surprises you, doesn't it? But think about it. There he is in the tightest cage ever created to hold a human being and he just walks out. He hits the callplate and tells them if they don't open up he'll mindwipe everyone in the building. I've never heard anything like it. We don't know if he can do it. He probably doesn't know if he can do it. But we can't take chances. We tried a few things to make sure he wasn't bluffing but ultimately, we couldn't tell so we had to let him go. You've got to admire that kind of style in a man, telepath or otherwise."

"If I see him, I'll pass along your admiration."

"If you see him, you call the police. Turn him in or the Bar Association will hear about it."

"McMasters, are you paying the bill for this call or am I paying for it as a taxpayer?"

McMasters grunted. "All right, Benson, but remember what I said—one sign of him and you call a cop."

Schwab heard the faint buzz of subspace static. Benson reached over and touched the phone. The static died. He looked up at Schwab. "McMasters is right. That was a dumb trick you pulled. How did you get here?"

"The same way you did, by starship. I even met the new governor. He complained to me about an escaped telepath."

Benson's face soured. "Don't get cute, Schwab. Anything like a chance you might have had walked right out of that cell with you. Unless you've got a damn good reason for showing up here, I'm going to call Finnley and let him have you."

Schwab tried to protest.

Benson interrupted. "Look, Schwab, you heard Mc-Masters. If they find out I didn't turn you over to the authorities as soon as I saw you, the Bar Association is going to have one word to say to me—out. They'll say you were a good lawyer, Benson, but not a man of honor. Moral turpitude, impropriety; whatever you call it, it will mean out for me and that isn't going to happen, not for you or anyone. I don't care what sort of extenuating circumstances you think justifies what you've done, but—"

Benson broke off, obviously distressed. When he continued, his voice was more controlled. "Now tell me, how did you get here and—more importantly—why?"

Schwab recapitulated his threat to the staff of the federation detention facility, his escape and the long trip from Earth. Benson, listening, grew progressively more astonished. Finally, Schwab reached the point in his tale where Benson saw him from the window.

Benson interrupted. "Okay, I get the picture. Now tell me the answer to the big question—why?"

"I told you, the footprints."

"What about them?"

"I had to come once I realized what they meant. I went over and over the whole thing in my mind and I kept asking myself whether I was guilty. I had mindwiped Morris but at the same time I still didn't think I had done what they said."

"We've been through all this before, Schwab."

"I know. I don't know how many times I went over it myself after you left, but it paid off. I remembered the footprints. Just before I was arrested in the tunnels, I came to a sort of intersection. The light was coming in through the vent hole over my head. I could hear the Parians coming closer and was about to start running again when I saw the footprints. At the time, I thought I must have been running in circles like they say people do. But they couldn't have been my footprints, Mr. Benson."

"Why?"

"Because after the concession guard arrested me, we walked back through the tunnels. We never crossed a place where there were more than two sets of footprints going the other way—mine and the guard's. I hadn't circled around at all."

Schwab noticed the smile on Benson's face, the first he had seen since entering the room. Was it just this new piece of evidence that made Benson smile? Or something more, Schwab's escape, his journey across space, never knowing whether a friend he had relied on was really a friend or would turn him in, a journey made on trust—and the reason for it? A footprint in a dusty tunnel.

"But why did you have to come, Schwab?"

"I thought to myself, they know Benson is here. If I just tell him about it, he still won't be able to do anything. The footprint was different than mine or the guard's. Someone has to go into the tunnels. You can't do it: if you disappeared from view too long, whoever's responsible would notice. But I could go into the tunnels. They'd be off guard."

"But whoever it is knows you're loose now."

"Does he know why? No."

"Okay, okay," said Benson, evidently giving in to Schwab's logic. "But tell me one thing. What—if you know—do you expect to find in those tunnels?"

"Regina Quinton."

Benson looked dubious.

Schwab answered Benson's question before he asked it. "I don't know why, Mr. Benson. But you haven't found her here in the concession yet, have you?"

"No," admitted Benson, his tone grudging. "No one seems to have heard of her. Or at least they say they haven't. But this plan of yours—going into the tunnels—is out of the question. If you go alone, there's no telling what will happen. We wouldn't have any way to communicate or coordinate our activities. If you get lost or—" Benson broke off, shaking his head. "I'm starting to think like you, instead of a court officer. What I should do is call Finnley and let him go into the tunnels with a squad of concession guards. If we go in on our own hook, without telling Finnley or anyone else in authority, it will amount to the same kind of impulsive, irrational action that brought you here. But will Finnley do it? The more I think about it, the more I suspect he won't do anything on his own, especially go into those tunnels. By the time he was through checking with his bureaucratic chain of command, half the concession would know what was going on. There is also a remote possibility that Finnley himself is involved." Benson looked up. "Just when did you want to start this little sewer search of yours, Schwab?"

Schwab smiled. "Early tomorrow morning there won't be any activity around the mounds or in the tunnels. I can slip out of the concession without being noticed."

"We can slip out," corrected Benson.

They prepared the room for sleep, planning to get as much rest as possible before the journey into the tunnels. Schwab—after the flip of a coin—got the bed and Benson the couch. The long Parian night would let them get nine hours of sleep before dawn.

Schwab, exhausted after the long day, fell asleep almost immediately. At first, his sleep was dreamless. Only toward morning did thoughts begin to surface, vague and amorphous thoughts. Slowly, after the long hours of sleep, his mind rose to the edge of wakefulness. Faint mixtures of impressions moved back and forth across his gradually increasing consciousness. The images of McMasters, Curly Curtis, the people who had helped him on the trip from Earth, Finnley and Benson. This last image remained— Benson on the couch as Schwab had last seen him. The impression, distinct and vivid, with none of the dreamlike quality of the earlier images, seemed to enwrap and fill Schwab's consciousness. It seemed to be trying, somehow, to reach the deepest recesses of his mind. Suddenly, Schwab recognized the sensation. He had felt it once before He saw Benson on the couch in front of him and realized he was standing next to the man. Through the haze, he could see Benson stir and begin to sit up. He could see Benson's mouth begin to move, forming a question. He could feel his own mind reach out, trying to make contact, trying to smother.

Schwab fought against the compulsion, his mind a dizzying whirlpool of sensation. He could see Benson—now fully awake—trying to lift himself from the couch. He felt the compulsion begin to overwhelm him. He struggled, his control slipping away. Just as his will was about to break, he saw Benson move, the lawyer's clenched fist coming up at him.

The blow hit Schwab squarely on the side of the jaw. He reeled, head thrown back, stumbling. He hit the edge of the bed and fell, losing consciousness.

Later, Schwab groaned and felt consciousness return. He blinked both eyes several times to clear them and looked around. He was on the floor. Benson, holding the phone like a large rock, sat above him on the edge of the bed.

"Just stay there, Schwab, until I'm sure you're all right."

Schwab looked around, mind still groggy. "What did I—"

"You tried to mindwipe me."

Schwab pushed himself up on one elbow, shaking his head vigorously from side to side. "No, I didn't—I didn't intend to—I mean, I fought against it."

"How do you feel now?"

Schwab looked up, his voice and face pleading. "Mr. Benson, I'm sorry."

"I asked how you felt."

"A little groggy. Otherwise, fine. It's you I'm worried about."

"Don't worry about me." Benson hefted the phone. "I'm protected."

Schwab looked at the phone. "All right, Mr. Benson, you have my permission. If you notice any sign of—" Schwab hesitated "—that sort of thing happening again, you can use that phone. Maybe you better use it anyway, not to hit me, but to call Finnley." Schwab looked up at Benson. "What am I, Mr. Benson? I did it to Governor Morris and now I almost did it to you—you, of all people, someone who's trying to help me. What kind of person am I?"

"Tell me what you felt. Maybe we can make something useful of that."

"I didn't feel anything. It was just like last time. I woke up and I found myself over you. I tried to struggle against it, but I couldn't. If you hadn't hit me, I would have done it. Mr. Benson, I can't be allowed to do these things. Call Finnley and tell him to send over the concession police and ship me back to Earth—or anywhere, even a rehabilitation center. If that will stop me, I'll accept it."

"We're not certain it's something in you, Schwab."

"We're not? Then why do I do it?"

"Did you do it on Earth?"

"No."

"Why?"

"I couldn't."

"That's right. Only here, on Paria. That seems significant to me."

"Maybe. On the other hand, I was never alone in the room with anyone who was asleep when I was on Earth. Both times it happened, I was with someone who was asleep. Maybe being on Paria is just a coincidence. Maybe whatever it is in me is only set off by that situation."

"Maybe. Are you all right now?"

Schwab shook his head. "I don't know. I don't know at all. I thought I was all right when I went to bed, but—" Schwab shrugged "—I wasn't. How am I supposed to tell?"

"Do you feel any of the sensations you felt standing over me?"

"No. But are you sure that's the key?"

"I'm not sure of anything, Schwab. But we have to play the odds."

"No, I don't feel the same way."

"Good. You can stand up now."

Benson put the phone on his lap and began punching out a long series of numbers.

"Who are you calling? Finnley?"

"Shh."

After several seconds of static, occasionally interrupted by audible clicks and beeps, the phone cleared. The number began to ring. Schwab heard someone answer and finally recognized McMasters's groggy voice. "What in hell's name is it now, Benson? Do you realize what time it is on Earth? It's four in the morning! Can't it wait?"

"I'm sorry about the time, McMasters. I'm still on Paria. I need some help."

"Help?" The voice sounded suspicious.

"This is important, McMasters. I wouldn't have called otherwise."

"All right, all right. Get it over with."

"I want a background check on—"

"At four in the morning!"

"I want a background check on three people, the head of mining operations here on Paria, a man named—"

"Cowdin. I talked to him briefly. Who else?"

"Max Jacobson. He runs the hotel here. And Governor Finnley."

"Finnley! That moron? Why do you—"

"He was on Paria when Morris was mindwiped."

"You're on the wrong track there, Benson."

"I'm not on any track. I'm just trying to cover all the bases."

"Benson, you can get a background check as easily as I can."

"Wrong. It would have to be worked up from scratch. My guess is you've already got one on Finnley, probably on Cowdin."

McMasters grunted. "Very shrewd, Benson. What are you onto?"

"Maybe nothing. I'll tell you later."

"Is that a promise?"

"Yes. If I get the background reports, I promise to tell you what, if anything, they lead to."

"Does that phone have a document feed on it?"

Benson glanced at the phone. "Yes."

"Just a second."

A pause ensued. Schwab could hear noises from the phone, including the voice of McMasters's wife complaining about being awakened in the middle of the night. Eventually, McMasters returned to the phone.

"Okay, Benson, I'll feed these through."

The document feed light on top of the phone came on. A long sheet of phonefax paper spilled out of the slot at the phone's base. When the light went out, Benson thanked McMasters, hung up, tore off the sheet and set aside the phone. He began studying the sheet.

"What are you looking for?" asked Schwab.

"I don't have the vaguest idea, but I'll know it when I find it."

Benson worked his way down the long sheet, nodding occasionally. Finally, he handed it to Schwab, who was sitting in the room's only chair.

Finnley—the first report on the sheet—had indeed been on Paria at the time of the mindwiping. However, his movements had been eitirely accounted for; he was either touring the colony or remained holed up in his room with someone described as his "secretary." Furthermore, Finnley's psychological profile showed a man too irresolute for so deliberate and decisive an action as mindwiping, and there was no indication whatsoever of any telepathic ability. In fact, Finnley was described as being somewhat less sensitive than normal to the thoughts and feelings of others.

Cowdin, though also possessing no indication of any telepathic ability, showed a psychological profile as strong and decisive as Finnley's was weak. Schwab vaguely knew the man's name as that of someone who had almost single-handedly pushed through the development of the mining operation on Paria. How could such a man be anything but aggressive? With a profile like Finnley's, he would have accomplished nothing.

Schwab's attention was drawn away from the predictable psychological profile to Cowdin's personal history, especially the past few years of it. Cowdin had completely directed the construction of all Diversicorp facilities on Paria, particularly those having to do with the Parians. At one point, Cowdin had tried and abandoned a plan to telepathically communicate with the Parians. He had brought in several independent teams of telepaths in an attempt to make contact. Evidently, the Parian mind was too alien to the human mind to allow a useful contact. The project had been dropped.

Though interesting in itself, especially under the present circumstances, one other point about the Parian contact experiment caught Schwab's attention: the date. The telepaths had been brought to the planet at about the same time Benson's search showed Regina Quinton's arrival on Paria. If Regina Quinton was an emitter-telepath, Cowdin had a clear justification for bringing her to Paria, saying she would provide the human-to-Parian link once the other telepaths had provided the Parian-to-human link. The others had been unsuccessful. At that point, they had packed their bags and gone home. Had Regina gone home with the rest?

Schwab folded the printout and handed it back to Benson. He found the information in it reassuring. The momentary doubts he had had about himself disappeared. He had been right to come. The evidence they needed to refute the kineticorder was here on Paria. Their task now was to find it and present it to McMasters.

Schwab glanced at the printout in Benson's hand, then at Benson. "We'll have to go into the tunnels."

Benson nodded. "I think so."

"When is the best time?"

Benson glanced toward the window. "We have 15 or 20 minutes until sunup." He looked at Schwab. "I can't think of a better time."

CHAPTER 15

As they left the hotel and started out of the concession, Schwab could see the yellows and oranges of the sunrise silhouetting dark eruptions on the skyline: the Parian mounds. When they left the static field surrounding the concession, the air temperature dropped from the constant 22 degrees Celsius within the human colony to four degrees outside.

They changed direction slightly and headed for the nearest mound, the one Schwab had run to a month before. Neither man spoke. Schwab began to feel uneasy, his anxiety at entering the tunnels growing with every step. Intellectually, he knew going into the mounds was necessary, probably even vital to his defense. Emotionally, he experienced the return of a horror he had originally felt during his desperate flight. Momentarily, the feelings overwhelmed him.

"Mr. Benson, I've changed my mind. I don't want to go in there."

They reached the base of the mound. Benson stopped and looked at Schwab. "Why?"

"I feel—I don't know, leery or something."

Benson's annoyance showed on his face. "Leery—what the hell is that supposed to mean?"

"I just feel like I don't want to go in there, ever. I can't explain it."

"Listen to me, Schwab. We're just beginning to get a break in this case. You're the one who came up with the idea, you and your footprint. I've done some checking.

I'm beginning to have a vague idea of what's going on. You saw McMasters's check on Cowdin. I don't know all the details yet, but I will. We have to go into those tunnels to find them."

"I know that, but I feel—"

"I want you to do something. I want you to examine your feelings closely. Tell me if your fear of the tunnels has any rational basis."

Schwab thought a moment. "The creatures, the Parians—"

"Are relatively harmless, at least as far as we know."

"Yes, but—"

"They frightened you when you were ignorant of their habits. Now you know more about them."

"What are you getting at?"

"You've been involved in two mindwipe situations. Both times, your motives in going to the person who was to be the subject of the mindwipe were vague, more like impulses, or dream motives that you can't exactly put your finger on but which compel you just the same. Are you with me?"

Schwab nodded.

"Now you don't want to go into the tunnels. And my guess is you can't come up with a reason."

Schwab examined his thoughts. Other than an amorphous fear of the tunnels, he could state no specific reason for not going into them. He nodded. "You're right. I can't, but—"

"Both descriptions of your motives could have been given by someone under hypnosis. I'm not saying we're dealing with anything like hypnosis in substance, but the effect may be somewhat the same. That means there might be a potential for something equivalent to post-hypnotic suggestion but in a telepathic context. You may have been given a suggestion to avoid the mounds and the tunnels."

Schwab thought about the explanation. It seemed to make sense. Even as he thought about it, his fear lessened, the unconscious suggestion weakened by a clear and conscious explanation. "Okay, I'll buy that."

"And assuming that's true, I think there's a way to use it to our advantage."

"What?"

"You may have been given a specific suggestion to avoid a particular area in the tunnels. If you have, your feelings of aversion will grow stronger the closer we get. If you feel anything like that, tell me immediately."

Schwab nodded. Benson was right. The possibility of something like post-hypnotic suggestion existed. Schwab's fears could then be used as a sort of homing device to lead them through the maze of tunnels. "All right, Mr. Benson. Let's go."

They started up the side of the mound. Schwab noticed that Benson let him lead. He wondered whether it was only because of the post-hypnotic suggestion possibility and Schwab's familiarity with this part of the tunnel network, or something else, some lack of trust. He recognized that Benson—whether he believed Schwab or not—would take no more chances with him after the attempted mindwipe. He could not blame the man for his caution.

During the climb, Schwab was upright at first. As the climb got steeper, he had to put his hands down into the loose dirt for balance.

Finally, they reached the crest of the mound. Had it been that steep the first time? Schwab felt apprehensive. If his memory had been inaccurate about how steep the mound was, how accurate would it be inside the tunnels, especially if Benson's post-hypnotic suggestion theory proved wrong?

Schwab looked down into the tunnel from the top of the mound and momentarily relived the terror of his first encounter.

Benson rested his hand lightly on Schwab's shoulder. "After you."

Schwab started down. His heels sank into the dull brown dirt, which soon overflowed his boots. Toward the bottom of the hole, the climb became steep again. They were forced to turn around to face the side of the shaft and back down. Benson, above Schwab, negotiated as best he could, trying to step where Schwab had stepped. Schwab moved carefully, searching with his foot for solid ground before he shifted his weight.

At last, sweating heavily and feeling the gritty film of dirt covering his skin, Schwab reached the bottom of the cone. He glanced over his shoulder once to the floor of the tunnel five meters below and pushed off, dropping the five meters and landing on his feet. His knees bent, absorbing the shock.

While Schwab waited for Benson to reach the floor of the tunnel, he peered down each of the underground passages. The tunnels seemed to be near freezing. They were dimmer than Schwab remembered, but would probably get lighter—and warmer—as the sun rose higher outside.

Benson, looking as grim as Schwab felt, dropped to the tunnel floor next to him, paused for a moment to catch his breath and then glanced around at the tunnels. "Which way?"

Schwab continued looking at the tunnels. The last time, he had entered them, his desperation afforded little opportunity to take his bearings. He had chosen at random, or what seemed at random.

Schwab shook his head. "I don't know."

"Which way were you facing when you landed the first time?"

Schwab peered in both directions. They seemed identical. "I can't tell. I just dropped to the floor and ran. I didn't think. I didn't try to remember anything."

"Try now."

"Mr. Benson, it's six of one and half a dozen of the other. I can't tell."

Benson thought. "All right, on the tape, you dropped through this air hole above us with your back to the wall of the cone; then you ran. We came down facing the cone." Benson turned around and pointed, indicating one of the tunnels. "That means we go this way."

They followed the direction Benson had indicated. Only occasionally did they have to stoop or turn sideways at narrow spots in the tunnel. They worked their way through the Parian corridors, built to accommodate two Parians abreast if necessary and with ceilings high enough to move objects larger than the Parians.

They arrived at the first intersection, dimly lit by small air holes above. Almost instinctively, Schwab chose one, starting into it.

"Schwab," said Benson behind him.

Schwab stopped.

Benson's expression looked worried. "Are you sure you know where you're going?"

Schwab could think of only one way to express it. "It feels like the right direction."

"Feels like it. You mean I was right about—"

Schwab shook his head. "No, I don't think so. I don't feel any apprehension. I feel more like we're going in the right direction. It's like I have a hunch and—"

"A hunch! We could follow your hunches halfway across the continent! If my idea's right, you have to start thinking in reverse. When your sensibilities say turn right, you turn left. That might get us someplace."

"If you're right. If you're wrong, doing it that way could lead us halfway across the continent, too. We don't even know what we're dealing with. How can we just guess at it? We can't. That means all we have to go on is my hunches, like the one that brought us down here in the first place."

Benson made some comment about wishing he had a piece of string to reel out behind him, then nodded. "All right. We'll do it your way for a while." Benson looked around at the tunnel walls. "But, frankly, I'm beginning to feel a little anxious myself. I've been looking at these walls. There isn't anything shoring them up. The roof could cave in any minute."

"The Parians have been building these tunnels since long before we were here. They probably know what they're doing."

Benson looked around at the walls, his expression dubious. "Probably."

"And I haven't seen any evidence of cave-ins."

"All right. They've been here this long. They'll probably last a little longer."

As they continued through the tunnels, Schwab thought about the other's misgivings. These were understandable. By now his sense of direction was guiding him deftly through the network. It continued to grow stronger each time they came to an intersection and Schwab had to choose a new direction.

"Mr. Benson, I think it's something more than a hunch. It may be some sort of spurious emission, like a transmitter broadcasting on a harmonic, but something I'm sensitive to. The closer we get—"

"Then we are getting closer."

"Yes. I think so."

"Good. I can see why you were confused the first time you came in here. All these tunnels look alike to me."

"We're getting closer," said Schwab. "I keep getting stray thoughts that can't be mine. Pictures of animals and an unsettling sense of having my feelings hurt. But they aren't my feelings."

"All right," said Benson, nodding. Schwab could see that what he had said made more sense to Benson than it did to him. "I take back everything I said about your hunches. We're on the right track. Let's go."

They continued walking, at last reaching an intersection of five tunnels, in an area the size of a large living room. The morning light outside seemed to drop slowly down the 30-meter shaft above them and had little effect on the chilly temperature. Schwab's breath formed visible clouds.

"This is as far as I got before, Mr. Benson."

"Find the exact spot."

Schwab searched the intersection floor, carefully examining the dirt for footprints. Unexpectedly, he came upon a well-worn path coming out of one tunnel and going into another. It was impossible to tell which direction was the one they wanted. Schwab chose without hesitation, starting into one of the tunnels.

"Wait a minute, Schwab. What's that smell?"

Schwab stopped and consciously inhaled the cold air. He knew the smell immediately. He had been paying so much attention to his inner promptings that he had neglected to remain conscious of the immediate surroundings. "It's the Parians."

They stood at the mouth of the tunnel, both listening intently. Schwab felt his uneasiness return. He began to hear the scraping noises the Parians made. The fetid smell grew stronger. Again, it was impossible to tell the direction of either sounds or smell.

"Mr. Benson, I made a mistake. Let's get out of here."

"Can you get us out?"

"I don't know. I can get us away from them."

"Can you get us around them?"

"What do you mean, around?"

"An alternate route, one that avoids the Parians."

"How can I? I don't know where they are."

Benson thought for several moments. Finally, he looked at Schwab. "Do you remember that section in McMasters's report about using telepaths to try and contact the Parians?"

"The attempt failed."

"Why?"

"How am I supposed to know?"

"Probably because the Parians' minds were too alien for the human telepaths. But we don't want direct communication. All we want to know is their location."

"Mr. Benson, I can't—"

"How do you know you can't?"

"I just can't. I've never tried."

"There's always a first time."

Schwab thought about the idea. He had no confidence in his ability to make contact with a Parian mind, or even of the results he might get from such a contact. "Mr. Benson, I don't think I can do it."

"Try."

"How?"

Benson shrugged. "You're the telepath."

Schwab considered this statement less than helpful. Still, they had nothing at all to lose—except time—by giving it a try.

Schwab closed his eyes. Mentally, he envisioned the tunnels and the Parians, wondering as he did whether the clear image in his mind came from his memory of the earlier events in the tunnels or the beginning of an actual contact. He relaxed, trying to give a full sensory range to the impressions, sight, sound, scent—scent! Abruptly, Schwab smelled an overwhelmingly vile odor, an alien and repulsive odor. He felt his stomach retch, nausea and repulsion setting in. "Mr. Benson?"

"What?"

"They smell us. It's strong. There's no way we can avoid them. They can find us by that horrible smell. I've never smelled anything like it."

"Where are they?"

"I told you, they'll find us, Mr. Benson."

"But we might be able to avoid them for a short time—long enough."

Schwab let the alien sensations play across his mind. Along with the sense data—the look of the tunnels through Parian eyes, the meaningless impression of the noises he and Benson made to Parian ears, and the smell, the overwhelming smell—something else emerged, a pattern, complex and intricate, yet clear and laden with significance—the tunnel pattern with all its philosophical and religious meaning intact. The pattern became clearer to Schwab's mind, each twist and turn of the network adding more meaning to the overall design.

"It's beautiful, Mr. Benson."

"What?"

"I never thought they were capable of anything that moving."

"What are you talking about, Schwab?"

"The Parians. Mr. Benson, we have to leave here. We are desecrating their work. By just being here, we are profaning what they have done. We have to leave, now."

"Not yet. We haven't found what we—"

Abruptly, Schwab turned and started back the way they had come.

Benson caught up with him. "Schwab, listen—"

"We have to go, Mr. Benson."

Benson grabbed Schwab's arm and jerked him around. "Schwab, we're not going. We've come this far. I'm sorry if we're invading the Parians' lives, or whatever it is you think we're doing, but we have to go on. If the Parians can do what you say they can do, they must have a concept like justice. In the name of that—"

"They don't think in those terms, Mr. Benson."

"Break contact with them."

"No, I can't. I—"

Suddenly, Benson's hand shot out, his open palm slapping hard across Schwab's face. Schwab's head recoiled, the image of the Parian mind instantly gone, the delicate contact broken.

Schwab blinked several times, clearing his head and beginning to feel his stinging cheek.

Benson continued to stare at Schwab's face. an inquiring look on his own face. "Are you—"

Schwab nodded. "I'm all right."

"Can you remember anything about the tunnel layout?"

"I think so." Schwab paused. "We have to go that way first."

They hurried in the direction Schwab indicated. Every step he took into the tunnel was like a revelation. Before the contact with the Parian mind, he had felt bewildered by the tunnels. Now, they opened new meanings at every turn. He found it impossible to verbalize. He led Benson through complex twists in the network, through narrow passages, including one that required them to crawl on all fours. Expertly, they circumvented the Parians.

Leading Benson through the tunnels, Schwab had only one reservation. During his telepathic link, he had seen something else in the aliens' minds, the image of a man. To Schwab, the significance of the man seemed disproportionate and exaggerated, as though the man had somehow become part of Parian life, yet remained apart from it. It was the only human who had any meaning in terms of the Parian system of thought. The man had no Parian name, yet Schwab knew the Parians would obey him. He was the man who took away the useless material when a new tunnel appeared.

Gradually, the tunnels widened again. They reentered the main body of the network. Their detour around the Parians would give them only a few extra minutes. Once the Parians caught up, he and Benson would have to begin another flanking maneuver or quickly reach their destination.

Benson tugged at the back of Schwab's shirt. "Are you sure you know where we're going? I've been through so many of these, they all look alike to me. And look at these floors No one's been in here but the Parians."

As they had distanced themselves from the Parians, Schwab's original sensation of a strong hunch had returned, had grown constantly stronger. As he was about to answer Benson's question, the hunch crystallized into something even firmer—words At first it came as an intermittent mumbling, faint and irregular. Then in a steady stream.

.   not acting good   escaped from a prison. I do not like that And Mr Cowdin says we have failed in our attempt to make him act good. He says the equipment worked perfectly That means he blames it on me. He thinks I did not do what I always do. He is wrong. I cannot help doing what I do. I wish I could not do it. I wish I was normal. I wish I did not have to live here. Still, he blames me. That is probably why he left. He said the contact broke and he blames that on me. I want to do what is right. I did not break the contact. Yet, he blames me. He has left to go out there with those horrible creatures. I do not like those creatures. I do not like being here.

Schwab gestured toward a narrow passage. "It's this way, Mr. Benson. I'm positive."

They walked through a short narrow passage and stepped into a wider, more frequently used passage. Human footprints showed in the dirt on the floor. At the end of the passage, 30 meters ahead of them, stood a door.

CHAPTER 16

So human and familiar an object as a door in so alien an environment unnerved Schwab. They walked to the end of the passage and stopped before it.

Schwab glanced at Benson. "What do we do now?"

Benson laughed slightly. "Open it, of course."

Schwab reached out and touched the lockplate, expecting the door to remain closed. Instead, it slid open, whishing faintly.

Cautiously, they stepped partway inside.

Again, the familiar assaulted Schwab's senses, but in an inappropriate mixture. The room looked like a cross between a data-processing center and a young girl's bedroom. Schwab stepped farther inside, looking curiously around. The wall to his left was composed of computer memory banks and analog circuits, all of it—laser memory blocks and banks of readouts—familiar from his experience on starships. Only the equipment near the end of the wall looked unfamiliar. He recognized something that looked like the kineticorder scanner he had seen on Earth, but without the scanning head. In place of the scanning head, a thick cable led off to the right.

Against the opposite wall stood a master console unit with a giant stuffed panda bear leaning against it. On top of the equipment stood rows of glass bric-a-brac, animals of some sort. Schwab recognized them from the two mind-wiping attempts and the faint emanations he had at first felt in the tunnels. The computers themselves were hung with frilly curtains.

Schwab's attention returned to the kineticorderlike equipment, most of it incomprehensible. His eyes followed the thick cable to a couch, where it disappeared. There he found the most unsettling sight of all—Regina Quinton.

Regina sat on a couch that sloped up at one end to a gigantic cushion for her gigantic head. She covered it almost completely. Her enormous body threatened to spill over the edges. Her hair was combed simply without any thought to design, only keeping it out of her eyes. Her face, puffy with fat, seemed to run down and blend with her neck, then disappear into the collar of her dress, a bulky black sack, as shapeless as its owner. Her legs were stretched out on a large circular cushion. The part that Schwab could see—from just below the knee to the thick heeled shoes—was white, fat and blue-veined.

Regina stuffed a bonbon in her mouth and swallowed it almost without chewing. She looked from Benson to Schwab and back to Benson. When she spoke, her thick lips barely showed movement. *Don't hurt me.*

Benson pushed past Schwab and approached Regina, pausing in front of the couch to look at her. Schwab could see in Benson's expression that he had decided she was of no immediate danger to them. Benson walked back to the computer console and began examining it.

Schwab kept looking at Regina.

She scowled back, pouting. *You are that mean Ernest Schwab, aren't you?*

Schwab started to deny the accusation, but Benson interrupted. "Come over here, Schwab, and look at this."

Schwab walked to the console. "What is all this, Mr. Benson? And that girl—"

Benson looked up from his examination of the computers, his fingers still on the console. "If we were on Earth, I would say this was a kineticorder installation, or something enough like it to be a twin brother."

"What do you mean, a twin brother?"

Benson waved Schwab into silence. "Just a second."

"But—"

Benson turned to Regina. An expression of demanding authority came onto his face. He repeated Schwab's question, snapping it out in a fierce voice. "What is all this equipment?"

Schwab could tell by Benson's tone that the abrasive force he used toward the helpless fat woman was a posture, a pose to elicit information, more as if Benson were badgering a witness on cross-examination than actually angry. Regina, a stranger to Benson, evidently interpreted it as hostility. Her eyes blinked, squeezing out a tear that rolled out over her round cheek and fell to her dress.

It is how we make people like him—she turned her eyes on Schwab, then looked back at Benson—*and you act nice to other people.*

Schwab could hear Regina's voice, clear and almost feminine in the distinct way every word was formed, yet her lips moved only slightly. Gradually, he realized she was not speaking at all. Her lips moved with the words as some people's do when thinking or reading, but the sound was entirely inside his head.

"How do you make people nice?" pursued Benson, his tone as angry as before.

Schwab understood, as he watched Regina, how the guards in the jail on Earth had felt about him when he demanded his release and threatened to mindwipe them. Here was someone actually capable of doing it. "Mr. Benson, don't get her excited."

"Quiet, Schwab," snapped Benson and returned his attention to Regina. "How? Tell me how you make people—" Benson glanced at Schwab "—him act nice."

Tears were flowing steadily from Regina's eyes. *I go to sleep and help Mr. Cowdin.* Her voice in Schwab's head, contradicting her facial expression, had none of the hesitant quality he expected. It remained clear and distinct without any undertone of fear. *You are not a nice man either. I do not like you. I am not going to tell you anything.*

Benson glared at her and took a step forward. "Regina, if you don't tell us, I am going to do something awful to you."

A look of utter horror came over Regina's face, the emotion reflected in a wave of horror from her mind.

Benson took another step toward Regina. "Regina—"

Don't hurt me.

"If you tell us what we want to know, we won't hurt you."

Regina pouted, sulked and scowled.

Benson raised one hand, as though about to slap her.

No! No! I will tell you. Don't hurt me! I go to sleep and Mr. Cowdin uses the equipment to make people act nice. I wish he were here now to make you act nice, you evil, evil man.

Schwab stared at Regina, incredulous. "I can't believe it, Mr. Benson. He uses her as some sort of telepathic transmitter. But the equipment, what is it for?"

"I'd guess he uses it both to amplify her telepathic emissions and to modulate them with whatever suggestion he wants to implant in people's minds."

"But why did he use me? I don't even know him. Who is he?"

"BENSON!"

The unexpected voice from the tunnel startled Schwab. He looked around at the open door.

"That," said Benson, nodding toward the doorway, "is probably our Mr. Cowdin. I would guess he's not alone. I think it's time to close the door, Schwab."

As Schwab touched the plate, then twisted it to the lock position, he could see Parians crowding into the tunnel outside, their large bodies jostling against one another. Scraping sounds, along with faint gruntings, issued from them. He saw no sign of the man, Cowdin. He remembered the man-figure from his contact with the Parians' mind. The Parians would obey him.

The door slid into place.

Schwab looked around. Benson had returned to examining the equipment. It seemed to Schwab they had more important things to do with their time. "Mr. Benson, what are you doing? That maniac is out there with God-knows-how-many Parians and you're still poking about that equipment."

Benson ignored the protest, saying only, "I think I can operate this."

"Who the hell cares? If I had to, I could operate a space shuttle manually, but that isn't going to get us out of here. What we should be doing is hunting for the back door."

"There isn't one. I checked."

"But—"

"Please be quiet, Schwab. Let me think this through."

Benson continued examining the equipment, nodding occasionally and emitting "ahs" as he worked his way across the console. Finally, he began examining the kineticorderlike equipment.

"Mr. Benson," said Schwab, anger and fear mixing in his voice, jabbing his index finger toward the door, "that man's out there cutting us off. We have to do something about him before he does something about us."

Benson nodded and spoke without looking away from the computer console. "Good idea. Keep him busy."

"Keep him busy! How the hell am I supposed to do that?"

Benson waved away the protest. "That's up to you. I've got my hands full. Throw something at him if you can't think of anything better." Benson looked up a moment. "No, strike that. Throw something at the Parians. They won't know whether you're throwing a bomb or food. Keep them busy and you'll keep Cowdin busy."

Schwab glanced around the room for something to

throw. His eyes fell on the giant panda. In desperation, he scooped it up and started for the door. A wave of hysteria issued from behind him.

MY PANDA!!!

Schwab heard Benson's calming voice. "Regina, it's all right."

Schwab reached the door and twisted the lockplate. The door slid back. Two snouts, enormous and murine, snorted and tried to push their way in. Two sets of glistening black eyes swiveled slightly and looked at Schwab. He held the panda bear under the arms and shook it at the Parians.

The eyes swiveled, as though the creatures were thinking. They snorted and began to back away. Schwab advanced on them with the bear.

"It's working, Benson."

"Good. Keep at it."

Just as the Parians had completely backed into the tunnel, a third creature appeared. Its great rodent mouth opened, showing three rows of sharp teeth, and clamped on the leg of the bear.

Schwab released the panda and slapped the doorplate with the flat of his hand. As the door closed, he saw the frenzied Parians tearing into the stuffed bear. Cotton stuffing spilled from the center of the panda. Schwab felt a chill go up his spine. He shivered once. The door closed.

He looked around for something else to throw and saw Benson at the console. Benson's fingers moved from plate to plate, the readouts casting an eerie array of colors— reds, yellows, greens—on his face. Just beyond Benson, Regina lay asleep, a used transdermal syringe on the floor next to her.

"Mr. Benson, what are you—"

"Dammit, Schwab, shut up! I told you to keep them busy. That's your job. This is mine."

"But—"

Benson looked around, his face—illuminated by the

moving patterns of light—infuriated. "Schwab, do as I tell you. I need a minute, maybe two. The more agitated those creatures are, the more agitated Cowdin will be. I don't want him to be able to think for at least the next two minutes."

Benson turned back to the console before Schwab could say anything. Schwab looked around for something else to throw. Since Benson was using the equipment, only Regina's possessions were left. Methodically, Schwab collected a pile of stuffed animals and glass figurines by the door. When he thought he had a large enough supply, he grabbed the closest one—a flop-eared veltor—and touched the doorplate.

The door slid back. The tunnel was literally filled with Parians, their odor making him retch once. He began throwing out stuffed animals. Knots of Parians crowded around each animal, teeth sinking in. When he ran out of stuffed animals, he began throwing the figurines. Glass shattered at random intervals along the tunnels. The Parians, confused for the first time, began losing their sense of purpose, milling in disorganized groups and backing away from the door. Schwab continued tossing the figurines, choosing the larger ones first.

When his stockpile began to run low, Schwab glanced over his shoulder at Benson, about to ask whether he could close the door. As he did so, the lights on the console died in front of Benson.

Benson looked at Schwab. "He's cut the power to the equipment. You can close the door now."

Schwab touched the plate, waited for the door to close, then twisted it to the lock position. He heaved a sigh of relief and looked at Benson. "What now?"

"Now," said Benson, looking as weary as Schwab felt, "we wait."

Schwab looked past Benson at Regina. "What about her?"

"Let her sleep. Those things you threw in the tunnel were hers. It would probably just upset her to know it. Plus, if Cowdin finds a way in here, none of us are going to leave. She doesn't have to know about that either."

"What were you doing with the equipment?"

"Just playing a hunch." Benson sat down on the floor, leaning his back against the computer. "I think we'd better skip talking and moving. This place only has a limited quantity of air and we'll need all we can get."

Schwab looked around at the room. He was about to comment that the air-conditioning seemed to be working properly, when the lights went out. He heard the last faint throb as the air-conditioning motor came to a halt.

He sat down opposite Benson, his back to the wall. "How long will we have to wait?"

"I don't have the vaguest idea—an hour, a day, a week."

"A week!"

"Unless we run out of air first."

"Mr. Benson—"

"Just stay calm. There's nothing else we can do."

"What about the door?"

"What about it?"

"He can open it. Shouldn't we do something? Put up some kind of barrier so we'll know he's coming if we're asleep?"

"We won't have to worry about that. He can't get in as long as the power's off. If he turns it on to come in, the lights will go on. We'll have some warning."

"For all the good it will do us."

"You're wasting air," Benson said.

"And I'm going to waste a little more. If I'm to die in this place, I'll die knowing what it was all about. You seem to have things pretty well figured out."

"Okay. You deserve that much. In my opinion, Cowdin is crazy."

"I could have guessed that much."

"For some reason, the particular form of his insanity attached itself to the Parians. It could have expressed itself in a multitude of ways. It happened to be the Parians. He identifies with them as expressing the proper order of the universe—all working together harmoniously toward a common end. Men, of course, don't work that way. That could be one of the reasons we're on Paria and the Parians haven't even got above the ground, much less off it. Be that as it may, Cowdin sees them as representing the perfect order. I doubt he actually knows what they are like. You, after your contact, probably have a clearer picture than he'll ever have."

Schwab thought about the brief contact with the Parians. Their view of the universe, in many ways more passive than humanity's, had much to recommend it. That they had developed no technology took little away from their achievement. Even among human beings, only the Occidental tradition had produced technology. The Oriental tradition had preferred to look inward, to build within man.

"Go on, Mr. Benson."

"I think he wanted, ultimately, to impose as much of the Parian system on mankind as possible, using Regina. Governor Morris was trying to close Paria to humans. That would have cut Cowdin off from his Parians and completely nipped his plan in the bud. He had probably been using Regina to influence decisions, planting a suggestion here, manipulating facts in someone's mind there. But Morris was strong-willed. He made his decisions only by objective, empirical facts. Empirical facts don't go away simply because a suggestion has been planted that they don't exist. When you showed up in orbit—by the way, Cowdin had access to your personnel file—he deduced you might be a low-grade receptor telepath from the indications in your file. He had had considerable experience with telepaths during his communication experiment with the Parians. He saw a chance to boost the power output and use you as a sort of relay to mindwipe Morris. You also provided a convenient scapegoat. That's about it."

"What about this equipment?"

"I think it implants, rather than extracts, thoughts. It's like the kineticorder—or, more exactly—like the mind probes we were not allowed to use in the judicial system. Regina is conditioned almost as intricately as the computer is programed. Cowdin must have done that the first time he used this with her."

Schwab leaned back against the wall and thought about what Benson had said. It gave him cold comfort.

They waited. Hours passed. Several times, something thumped against the outside of the door, Parians, or perhaps Cowdin. Each time he heard noise at the door, Schwab raised his eyes to the ceiling, expecting the lights to go on. How would it happen? Would the light come on, blinking, then followed by the opening of the door, the rancid odor of the Parians and a rush of gray bodies through the narrow opening? Would they have time to fight at all? Even if they did fight, would anything they did be effective against the creatures?

Schwab tried to relax and conserve air. Cowdin might simply wait them out, a war of attrition. They would starve slowly or run out of air instead of dying quickly.

As the time passed, Schwab began to lose track. Whether they had been there five, ten or 15 hours he was unable to tell. In addition, his sense of balance and direction were becoming disoriented by the total blackness. Once, when he said something to Benson, the direction Benson's answer came from startled him. If Cowdin could find some way to open the door in the dark, they would have no chance at all.

Later, Schwab began to hear the scraping. He had difficulty telling its direction. He felt his way along the floor, fingers at the intersection of wall and floor, until he reached the door. He put his ear to the metal. He could hear the scraping clearly. Someone or something was working at the other side of the door.

The scraping lasted for approximately 15 minutes, then, abruptly, stopped.

"Mr. Benson, do you smell anything?"

"No."

"Are you sure?"

Benson hesitated before answering. "No."

"I distinctly smell something, but I can't tell where it's coming from. It seems to be all around me."

A jarring, wrenching noise came from the door. Schwab involuntarily pulled back. In front of him, the door blossomed into a head-sized hole. Light streamed through, making a spot on the floor.

"Got it!" someone shouted.

A face appeared in the circle of light, Governor Finnley's face, peering into the darkness. "Hello?"

"We're here," said Benson.

Finnley brought a handlight up by his face and clicked it on. The beam blinded Schwab. He heard Finnley's startled voice.

"You!"

EPILOGUE: BENSON

Benson felt like needling someone—anyone. He was impatient to leave Paria. His impatience made him irritable. His irritation made him want to needle someone.

Neither he nor Schwab had seen anything of Governor Finnley for the past two days. Benson had hoped, vainly, they would see nothing at all of him. He had hoped they would make it to their shuttle and lift off for the starship orbiting Paria before the governor realized they were gone. Finnley had interviewed Regina Quinton for his reports. He had probably talked to Cowdin at the Concession Security office. But he had talked to neither Benson nor Schwab during that time. The governor had even been absent when Regina left Paria to return to Wolff-74-5 after she was cleared of any charges. Only now, when they were preparing to leave, did Finnley appear in Benson's room. Consequently, Benson chose to needle Finnley. He did so by ignoring Finnley and packing the last of his clothes.

Schwab, in one of Benson's suits, was seated on the couch. The suit fitted him loosely but was cleaner—and more reputable-looking—than the clothes he had worn into the tunnels. Finnley was perfectly dressed in his official tunic, everything neat but his face, which reflected by its tight lips and blinking eyes that the mind behind it was worrying something to death.

Benson let Finnley worry and went on with his packing. Whatever it was would soon enough be out without encouragement. Besides, thought Benson, for some perverse reason, he enjoyed seeing Finnley agitated.

"Why," demanded Finnley when he could no longer stand the silence, "did you go down into those tunnels without contacting me? I was the proper person to handle the matter from the beginning! If you had contacted me and been perfectly frank, I would have come to the conclusions I did about Morris's papers long before you landed yourself into that mess. Do you have any idea what Cowdin had on him when he was arrested? A nerver! If he'd gotten through that door, you would have been worse than mindwiped! Why, Benson, didn't you come to me?"

"We thought you'd figure things out."

"And lucky for you I did. You were right about that. But have I heard any thanks for it?"

"Thanks," said Benson.

"Thanks," said Schwab.

Finnley grunted, disgusted. "Go ahead, you two, make light of it. Without me, you would both be dead."

Benson closed his suitcase, sealed it and looked up at Governor Finnley, keeping his face as impassive as possible. "How did you happen to put things together so quickly, Governor? It was a very complicated matter and you seemed to cut right through all the superfluous material and get to the heart of it."

Finnley, mollified by Benson's tone, smiled. "You've put your finger right on it. That's exactly how it happened. I was standing in my office, thinking and pacing. Morris's papers lay on the desk, and I glanced at them at every pass. I had read them over and over without being able to make heads or tails of them. They were all about those giant rodents and their doings. I was standing there, musing, when suddenly it came to me. It was a striking experience. One minute I didn't have the vaguest idea what was going on. The next minute, there it was in my mind as clear as a bell—Benson and Schwab are trapped in an underground room in the Parian tunnels with Cowdin outside trying to kill them. The insight was so clear and certain that I immediately called the concession police and formed a search party. Strange, isn't it, how insights like that just appear in people's minds."

"But—" began Schwab.

Benson frowned, cutting off Schwab. "Well, Governor, there's no accounting for the way some minds work."

Finnley nodded solemnly. "True, true. We may not all be telepathic—" Finnley gave a significant glance at Schwab "—but there are compensations with other mental faculties." Finnley stood up. "Well, Benson, I must go. My duties call."

Finnley shook hands with Benson and Schwab, then left.

When the door closed, Benson, still in a mood to needle someone, glanced at Schwab. "The question now is what we're going to do with you."

"Me?"

"You may not have mindwiped Morris but you did escape from jail. That sounds like a felony to me."

"But I had to. You know that."

Benson remained silent, letting Schwab work himself up. Schwab continued protesting both his innocence and the necessity of his escape for several minutes. Only the glowing phone interrupted.

Benson answered it.

McMasters's face peered soberly out. "Ah, Benson, I'm glad I caught you before you boarded. I've just read Governor Finnley's report on your health vacation. It didn't sound too healthy."

"I appreciate your concern. Do you have any other reason for spending tax money on this call?"

"Grumpy today, aren't we? I'll come to the point. We seem to have run into a problem with that Schwab man of yours." McMasters shook his head in what was obviously mock perplexity. "Heaven only knows I've done everything I could to nail the fellow to the wall, but, alas, I can't find a statute that covers him. I even considered assault and battery for a while, but I finally gave up on the idea."

Benson smiled. McMasters's failure to find an offense that covered Schwab had given Benson an idea of his own. Having rattled Schwab's cage for a while, he saw an opportunity to rattle McMasters's. "I don't really want to say anything, Brother McMasters, but weren't you on the Federation Penal Code Revision Commission?"

McMasters scowled. "Yes, yes, yes. The Revision Commission. You know I was, Benson. And when you get back here and people around the local bar association start asking you about it, you say you don't know who it was on that commission that recommended dropping the prison breach and escape statutes from the code. After all, Benson, we hadn't had one in 100 years. At the time, it seemed reasonable."

Benson agreed it seemed reasonable and glanced over the top of the phone at Schwab. Schwab appeared angry about something. For a man who had just discovered he had not committed a crime because the crime he believed he had committed no longer existed, Schwab did not seem to Benson to show the properly happy attitude. Who could he possibly be angry with? Benson?

Schwab, still angry, turned and left the room. Benson watched him. One thing was certain. Benson's job was finished. Angry or not, Schwab could go where he pleased. No one would try to stop him.

Read about more exciting titles on the next page

THESE LASER BOOKS STILL AVAILABLE
FOR ONLY 95¢ EACH

Read about more exciting titles on the next page:

No. 31 **Galactic Invaders** by James R. Berry
Almost single-handedly, Keith Cranston must thwart the sinister alien threat to the Earth Federation.

No. 32 **Then Beggars Could Ride** by R. F. Nelson
One man's bewildered pilgrimage through the ages in search of his own Utopia.

No. 33 **The Dreamfields** by K. W. Jeter
What is the sinister purpose behind the psycho-therapy experiments of Operation Dreamwatch?

No. 34 **Seas of Ernathe** by Jeffrey Carver
The mysterious sea creatures pose a dangerous yet puzzling threat to the people of Ernathe.

No. 35 **I, Aleppo** by Jerry Sohl
A team of research scientists stumble upon sinister dream creatures capable of ruthless murder.

No. 36 **Jeremy Case** by Gene DeWeese
The sole survivor of a plane crash finds himself possessed by a strange power.

USE THIS HANDY FORM TO ORDER YOUR BOOKS